John Sam Jones comes from Barmouth. He has worked as a teacher, a chaplain in hospitals and prisons and a sexual health worker, more recently coming back full circle to work for the education service in Denbighshire. His first collection of stories, *Welsh Boys Too*, was awarded a Gay and Lesbian Honor Book Award by the American Library Association.

He lives with his partner in a village on the Dee estuary.

Fishboys
of
Vernazza

John Sam Jones

PARTHIAN

Parthian
The Old Surgery
Napier Street
Aberteifi
SA43 1ED
www.parthianbooks.co.uk

©John Sam Jones, 2003
All rights reserved.

ISBN 1-902638-34-4

Typeset in Sabon

Printed and bound by Dinefwr Press, Llandybie

Edited by Gwen Davies

With Support from the Parthian Collective

Parthian is an independent publisher that works with the
support of the Arts Council of Wales and the Welsh Books
Council

British Library Cataloguing in Publication Data.
A cataloguing record for this book is available from the
British Library.

Cover Design: Jo Mazelis *from*
                 Marc Rees in *RevolUn*
                 photography by Huw Walters

For Jupp

Acknowledgements

Special thanks to Gwen Davies for editorial support &
to Federica Sturani for assistance with the Italian.

Stories

The Fishboys of Vernazza

Giacomo's knowing smiles and attempts to engage them in broken English don't entice them to dawdle in the Bar Gioia, not even with all the fidgety-fingered cradling of his crotch, as is the way of so many Italian boys. They know that the hike from Monterosso to Vernazza will take at least a couple of hours so they can't indulge in Giaco's flirting or linger over their sticky pastries and cappuccinos. If they miss the train they'll have to wait another hour and that will certainly mean they'll be cutting it fine. Shôn smiles his cheekiest smile and asks Giaco if he'll be behind the bar later.... And so it's agreed that they'll come back and drink *sciacchetrà* with him after they've eaten dinner.

From the gloomy station building that smells rancidly pissy, the passengers that alight the train spill onto the narrow, sun-soaked promenade. Geraint and Shôn stroll beneath the neatly trimmed oleanders, the leaf cover just thick enough to diffuse the sun's warmth and allow them to feel the autumn's chill. Every now and then, Shôn darts from the purple shadows and leans out over the balustrade to ogle the few dedicated sun worshippers that lie in skimpy trunks on Monterosso's sandy beach. Geraint would like to do the same, but it isn't in his nature to be quite so open about his attraction to other men. Knowing this, Shôn describes the delights that he sees (or just imagines) in clipped, crude morsels:

"Nice ass on that one…. Oh God, there's one over there who's got pecs to die for…. And this one here's got such a packet." Geraint feigns disdain at the teasing and wonders if Shôn has plans to cop off with some handsome Italian. Then, for a few minutes, he considers his place in Shôn's life, despite promising himself that he wouldn't allow such introspection to spoil their time together.

He doesn't like to think of himself as Shôn's fuck-buddy, though that's how Shôn describes their relationship whenever Geraint tries to pin him down. He considers it such a vulgar term, and so American… and it hardly reflects the reality of their nights together when mostly they just cuddle. He's Shôn's teddy bear really, but Shôn's image of himself is far too butch to allow for such a passive interpretation of their liaisons. Geraint doesn't know how much longer he'll let him continue to shape this part of his life. Monogamy and a joint mortgage on a three-bedroomed semi, preferably with a garden, is what he hankers for… a quiet and secure marriage. But they retain their separate lives, their separate flats, their separate circles of friends, and come together only once or twice a week, and for holidays, because that's what Shôn wants. So Geraint takes what he can get; after all, Shôn is a lot of fun to be with… he's gentle, kind and generous (which tempers the bitchy streak), and when a teddy bear to cuddle is the last thing on his mind, their sex is pretty accomplished. Shôn is the only man Geraint has ever loved. And in four years Shôn has never so much as whispered to Geraint that he loves him.

"What about him?" Shôn quizzes, pulling Geraint back from the edge of pensiveness.

"You're like a dog on heat," Geraint jibes.

The track ascends quickly through the terraced vineyards, taking them along uneven pathways that crown the dry stonewalls and up crude, steep steps that connect the terraces. The vines have been recently stripped and most have been pruned back ready for the winter, their few remaining leaves blotchy with red and gold. The grapes, the *albarola, vermentino* and the *bosco* wither and wizen in some shady spot, a vital step in the process of turning them into *sciacchetrà*. The trail takes them past isolated huts that defy the precipitous gradients with stubborn sturdiness. Around these now forsaken vinedresser's shelters, clumps of prickly pear rear up like tethered, menacing beasts, to deter the inquisitive rambler from exploring. Where the terraces have been abandoned and recolonised by native heathers and squat pines, the *maquis* has reclaimed the derelict refuges.

Above the vineyards, a sea of white crested turquoise a thousand feet below them, the path, though obvious enough, is rough. Gouged into the face of the mountain, the original course is obstructed time and again by boulders from rock falls. Where landslides have gashed the sea cliff's contours, haphazard cairns mark an imprecise direction across the rock fields.

"You'd think they'd have put a sign up about the condition of the path," Geraint carps.

"There was one," Shôn says dismissively, "but you've got to have a bit of adventure in your life. Besides, the Australians I was talking to last night when you were reading your book said they'd walked it, and once we've crossed the ridge we get back onto the terraces."

Where the vines begin again, the descent becomes vertiginous. Geraint stops every few minutes to curse his new varifocals and their tendency to blur the irregular steps unless he looks directly down at his feet. Pausing on a bluff, he takes in the view: Vernazza, hanging on its rocky spit around an almost circular harbour, looks like a child's model village, the pink and lemon and ochre of the tall, narrow, green shuttered houses adding to the toy-like quality. Shôn bounds on ahead and after ten minutes or more, Geraint finds him slouched against a rocky outcrop.

"What do you make of this, then?" Shôn asks, pointing at a carving in the rock face.

"Mermaids," Geraint quips with delight.

"That's what I thought, but…"

"Right… they're boys!"

"Exactly… three cute mermen. I wonder what it's all about?"

"Probably some local legend," Geraint shrugs. "The artist was no amateur."

"It's good, isn't it?"

They come into Vernazza by a lane behind the octagonal domed church, where washing hangs from clotheslines and spider plants hang low from balconies of potted scarlet cyclamen. They find the small terrace of the Ristorante Belforte at the top of the uneven steps at the end of the harbour wall, just like the fetching older couple they'd befriended on the train from Genoa had described: four tables, decked with pink linen cloths and napkins, polished silver cutlery and crystal glasses that glint in the glorious October sun. Shôn, his scientist's eye trained to observe the merest detail, gestures to Geraint that they should sit, as there's no evidence that the splashes from the waves can reach them. Despite Sol's benevolence since their arrival in the Cinque Terre, Neptune and his sirens have been irritable, the sea choppy... squally even; rough enough for the ferryboats that connect the five villages to have abandoned their erratic schedules and for the smaller fishing boats to have remained at anchor. Waiting for *il cameriere* - the waiter - whom the old queens on the train had said, with the campest affectation, was *molto delizioso*, they watch the translucent, azure waves rupture into cascades of glistening diamonds as they fold heavily onto the rocks not ten metres below them.

Between glances at the menu, Shôn takes in his surroundings. Over Geraint's shoulder he has a view of the harbour. The fishing boats, brightly painted in red and blue, are pitched by the swell, their short masts tracing the fingerprint whorls on the harbour cliffs where some ancient sea god's hands once moulded the strata. Wherever the rocks give way to vegetation, agaves cling like stranded starfish. Higher up, between prickly pears and heather, an errant bougainvillea bleeds its loveliness from a deep gash. And he thinks of Geraint, and whether he should commit himself.

With a lyrical *ciao*, the fingers of his left hand indolently sinuous at his crotch, *molto delizioso* interrupts Shôn's reverie.

Shôn studies the boy's felinity as he approaches their table. There's a grace in his movements that pleases the eye and suggests he might be a dancer. His arms, the muscles defined beneath a smooth chestnut shell skin, are strong; the sort that take your breath when they embrace you. The features of his face are more Abyssinian than Siamese, and framed by thick black hair, sleek and worn unfashionably long. His smile, in so proud a face, seems slightly mocking but there's a seductive stealthiness in the charcoal of his eyes that quickens Shôn's pulse. In a fleeting thought, Shôn concludes that Geraint, alongside one so dangerously desirable, is too safe... too dependable, and altogether too tame.

Between them they have enough Italian to recognise that there's a choice of local fish on the menu, but they enjoy the boy's attention and pretend to be stupid Brits abroad, coaxing him to translate *pulpo*, *totani* and *acciughe*. They ask for octopus and squid with potatoes *alla genovese* and freshly-caught anchovies with lemon. As he writes the order on his pad, Geraint notices the silver ring on the waiter's index finger.

"I've never seen anyone wearing a ring there before," Geraint says after *molto delizioso* goes back into the restaurant, rubbing the index finger of his right hand between the two end joints.

"It's called the middle phalanx," Shôn says, a bit like a lecturer in an anatomy class.

"Well... whatever... it's still a strange place for a ring."

"What's even more strange is the pattern and the figure engraved on it," Shôn scoffs.

"I didn't notice," Geraint submits.

The boy returns, places a rustic loaf of bread and a jug of wine on the table, and disappears again through the curtain of corded beads that keeps the flies out.

"It's a merman," Geraint offers, surprised.

As he clears their table, and just after he's asked if they want an *espresso*, Shôn asks him about the carving on the rock above the village.

"You mean the... fishboys?" he hesitates. "You call them

fishboys in *Inglese*?"

"It's a good enough name," Geraint quips.

"You been to the *grotta del Diavolo*?"

"The devil's cavern? No."

"Sometimes, when the sea is *tempestoso*, the fishboys come into the village through the *grotto*, and take away... how you say?" The charcoal embers in his eyes glow. "They take away the bad boys."

They laugh at his fishy tale and Shôn, catching his eye, teases, "And just how bad does a boy have to be to be charmed away by the fishboys?"

"Bad enough that... *lui è desiderabile*," he says with an inscrutable smile and carries the plates away.

"He's quite a story teller," Geraint says as the curtain of beads clacks. "Bad enough that you're desirable indeed!"

"He is pretty desirable," Shôn quips.

"Yes... and did you see how he hid the ring on his index finger in his hand when you asked about the carving?"

"I wonder," Shôn muses. "When he leaned over to pick up the plates his hair fell forward. He's got a strange mark behind his ear, all feathery and reddish-purple... just like a fish's gill."

They eat ice-creams on the *piazza* that fronts the harbour and then cross into the purple shade and take a narrow street made even narrower by stranded fishing boats, hauled from the sea for repair or a coat of paint. Geraint gawps at the large, ugly fish being laid on the marble slabs outside the *pescheria* by the fishmonger, fresh from his siesta. Shôn gawps at the fishmonger's apprentice, a tall, awkward youth with a cheeky smile. As the boy stands before the open refrigerated display counter arranging rose-coloured fish with golden streaks around a hand-written sign that reads *Triglia,* Shôn thinks that in a year or two, when he's filled out a bit, he won't be unattractive. The boy's hands are bloodstained and scaly and a silver ring glints on the middle phalanx of his right index finger... and when he turns, Shôn makes out the curious purple mark behind his ear. So the boy's potential has already been realised. Further up the street the cobbles are drenched in an arc of sunlight. Enjoying the warmth of the sun they peer into the *grotta del Diavolo*. Shôn wonders if the fishmonger's apprentice and the waiter put up much resistance when the fishboys of Vernazza lured them into the devil's cavern.

After a long shower, Shôn sneaks into bed beside Geraint, rousing him from his nap. They cuddle for a while and watch the sun set in a haemorrhaging sky and then they make love, their crazed delight inspired by their holiday mood, the gorgeous waiter and his fable. As their sex gives way to slumber, Shôn supposes that life with Geraint might be worth a try. Watching the last smears of blood fade into the gunmetal sky, Geraint decides it's time to get off the emotional roller coaster of the half-life he half shares with Shôn.

Later, at the Bar Gioia, Giacomo pours three stout goblets of *sciacchetrà*. The silver ring on the middle phalanx of his right index finger catches the light as he tilts the bottle. They raise their glasses, and swirling the richly amber, slightly viscous wine, they toast: "*Salute!*" Geraint's senses fill with curiosity and cocoa, apricot and Mediterranean herbs. Shôn is aroused by his lusty thoughts for Giaco.

"Is a very good one, no?" Giacomo enquires, his round, cheery face filled with pride. "Is the one my mother makes… much better than the one you buy in the tourist shop."

"It is very good," Geraint ventures, his gaze drawn and held in the questioning blue-green of Giacomo's eyes.

"You want to buy *sciacchetrà* you come see me before you go back England," Giaco says when he's peered too long into Geraint's confusion.

"We will," Shôn says stressing the *we*, jealous that Giaco seems more interested in Geraint.

Giacomo returns to their end of the bar after serving a giggly teenage couple.

"Can you tell us anything about the carving in the rock above Vernazza?" Geraint asks.

"We couldn't find anything about it in the guide book," Shôn says, competing for attention.

"I don't know," Giaco says with a shrug. "I never walked on this path."

"It has three fishboys, like the one on your ring," Shôn accuses.

Giacomo holds up his finger and looks, almost seriously, at the silver band.

"Is a very cheap ring from a shop in Spezia," he says, smiling. "Is very fashionable to have a ring here," he adds, rubbing the middle phalanx with his thumb.

For a while, they watch Giaco's every move as he serves more customers further along the bar. A larger than life, blonder than blonde girl sweeps into the Bar Gioia with smiles and *ciaos* for everyone. Shôn observes her carefully and deduces that she's the local transvestite. She rests her ample breasts on the bar and reaches over to kiss Giaco, ruffling his sandy curls with her crimson nailed fingers. Her skirt rises as she stretches. Geraint and Shôn are distracted by her black lace panties, which are too skimpy to hide her fishy tail.

Just Beyond the Buddleia Bush

Shifting the heavy Victorian chaise-longue hadn't been as straight forward as Eurig Dafydd had supposed; it had meant moving the formica topped table and the four mismatched dining chairs, and shoving the Welsh dresser over a couple of feet. He'd had to lift the rug too, because every time he lunged at the chaise it had ruffled and snagged around the carved oak legs. Twice he'd nearly given up and, slumping into the solace of the chaise's worn leather, he'd wondered whether he might not leave the damn thing where it was; where it had stood for twenty odd years because Fflur had liked the view across the strait towards Caernarfon and the mountains. But Fflur wouldn't be coming back to *Cwningar*. She'd settled for the house near Rhos in their quite amicable divorce and taken up with a new boyfriend, some doctor from Chester with an annual membership at an exclusive health club that entitled them both to sun-beds, saunas and squash. No more rambles with a Collins pocket flora for Fflur... no more midnight swims in Malltraeth Bay or beachcombing along Newborough Sands. She'd joined the Cheshire set.

Eurig had always preferred the view from the French window, where the three peaks of the Rivals scraped the sky beyond the acres of dunes and the sea, and where a path, just beyond the buddleia bush, cut its way through the August carpet of thrift and common sea lavender in the dune slacks, leading to the secluded beaches near Abermenai Point. With a final shove, he repositioned the chaise and from this new vantage point, lying on the cool leather to catch his breath, he watched two peacocks and a common blue in a complicated dance around the butterfly bush. After some time, the equally intricate moves of two boys, cruising one another as they made for the beach along the path, absorbed his attention. One of them reminded him of Seimon, and lest he should feel again the stab of his oldest son's words, he sought to distract himself and attended to the rug that he'd slung over the back wall to air in the morning sun.

But Seimon's hard words began to echo around him and Eurig wondered how long it would be before they'd be able to talk it all through, without tantrums and abuse. Damn the golden haired boy for reminding him so vividly of Seimon! Had it been Hefin who'd responded with such hostility, Eurig would have been less surprised and perhaps not even cared too much; after all, Hefin had always been a bit of a Mammy's boy and taken Fflur's side in everything. But no... Hefin had shown an understanding of the human condition's curiously fickle nature that seemed beyond his fifteen years. Fflur had suggested that perhaps Seimon's disappointment was the greater because he and Eurig had been so close — and that his feeling of betrayal, therefore, was that much deeper. In that sense, Eurig could see how Seimon had, perhaps, lost considerably more than Hefin had, and that was why he needed to try to talk with him again.

After vehemently beating the dust of many months from the rug, releasing within its cloud some of the upset and frustration that had built up in the days since the row with his head-strong seventeen year-old, Eurig rolled it back over the living room floor and moved the table and dining chairs back to their place. He took in the new layout and was pleased. Now that "The Warren" was no longer just for the odd weekend and summer holidays he needed to put his own stamp on the cottage. After much hassle he'd had the phone connected, and in time he'd replace the eccentric remnants that had accumulated over the year: curtains no longer matching changes of wallpaper in the family home and chairs too dated or loose-springed for everyday comfort. Eurig knew that when he came to chop them into sticks for the stove, each piece of furniture would surrender its bittersweet memories.

Eurig

With the grandfather clock's choked mid-day chime, you consider the promise of the dunes and relish the afternoon's possibilities. You strip. Rubbing the factor twenty sun block into your thighs and up into your groin, you become aroused at the prospect of meeting Dylan again. Catching sight of yourself in the cracked mirror of the wardrobe door you wonder whether to smear your pidyn with sunscreen; you certainly don't want to get burnt there. You lick your forearm, already covered with sun lotion; it tastes unpleasantly chemical. You'll just have to risk sunburn if you take off your trunks!

They'd met the previous afternoon. After an unsuccessful hour cruising a twenty-something, muscle-bound god with a conch-shell tattoo where others might have an appendix scar, Eurig had given up the chase. Lying on his towel in a shallow hollow, his head cupped in his hands, he mused on what might have been. Dylan, attracted by the genial look of an older man, sat on a low dune, partly concealed by a tussock of marram grass, and watched Eurig for a good ten minutes; he took in the leanness of his body, the greying at his temples and the black thickets in his armpits and groin. He feasted on the fantasy of their bodies coming together... but the pips from his watch broke through the reverie and signalled that his time in the dunes was up for another day. Eurig smiled at the man whose watch alarm had drawn his attention, and though he was unable to make out his features in the bright sunlight, he beckoned him over. They shook hands rather formally, Eurig thought, given that so many in the dunes were considerably more intimate on an altogether anonymous basis. They introduced one another, and as Dylan explained that he had to get back to the hospital for an evening clinic, Eurig lost his head in the boy's searching gaze.

Eurig
Still captured in the virid depths of Dylan's eyes, you lie back into the warm, soft sand beneath your towel and enjoy the random collision of thoughts. His tanned skin inviting your touch... the affectionate smile that drew you in... the unfashionably long hair, bleached by the sun and the sea's saltiness. And from the Mabinogi tales of your childhood comes the fabled Dylan Ail Môr, and Dylan becomes your child of the sea, within whose beauty you swim — until the shadow cast by a stranger dims your visions. The conch-shell tattooed boy stands over you, offering himself. Recognising that Dylan has stirred your emotions, you send the boy, by now quite confused and disappointed, on his way — and you dive back deeply into Dylan's sea.

Dylan
Showering quickly before changing into your uniform, you try to resist the lure of a sexual fantasy with the man in the dunes. He said his name was Eurig. An unusual name, but hardly a golden boy... but that's all right; you like the greying, older, slightly tarnished look. You doubt that he's much more than forty and ten years isn't such a gap. Perhaps his heart's golden? He seemed so mannerly, shaking hands and all; such courteousness is rare amongst the dune cruisers. You try to conjure in your mind the friendly face attached to the body that has so turned you on, but the features are ethereal and quietly you concede that your mind is a bit one-tracked when it comes to the physical features of men. Yet it was something in Eurig's face that had deepened your interest. How tired his eyes looked, perhaps? Maybe there was some sadness in the face, too. Pulling on your trousers, you wonder if Eurig might not turn up the next day. The melancholy brought on by this doubt un-nerves you. You question the spell

cast over you by Eurig's smile, which comes with transient vividness to your mind's eye.

Eurig
Passing through the gate by the buddleia bush, you consider the possibility that Dylan might stand you up; after all, you barely exchanged more than a dozen words. How was it possible that he'd aroused such a cauldron of feelings? How could you have been so stupid, so adolescent even, to have been seduced by those green eyes and allowed yourself to believe that he might actually fancy you? You push off the bleakness of the disappointment you foresee descending, should Dylan decide to stay away. You seek, instead, to occupy yourself in a search for the spear-leaved orache and viper's-bugloss that grow along the path amongst the thrift.

Dylan
You try to ignore the fact that you're being cruised and hope that the man who circles the rim of the hollow will leave you alone. The last thing you want, if Eurig does turn up, is for him to think you're copping off with someone else. When the gym-sculptured parody finally comes down into the hollow and struts his stuff, you recognise the boy with the conch-shell tattoo. With a smile, you ask if the antibiotics you'd prescribed him at the clinic the previous week have done their job and whether the crab lice you'd found in his groin and armpits are still driving him crazy at night. You don't catch the boy's reply as he runs off over the brow of the hollow.

Eurig
You wonder only fleetingly why the cupid with the conch-shell seemed so flustered as he pushed past you along the path where the marram grass seemed especially spiky on the back of your legs. Catching sight of Dylan in the hollow, sitting on a bleached tree-trunk worn smooth by un-logged voyages in the Irish Sea, your mind races. Might yesterday's mirage be exposed in the glare of a

new day's sun as no more than a brazen dune bum, randy for anonymous intimacy? Do your baggy shorts betray the sexual desire that quickens your breathing? Will you still find yourself in love, or be stung by your crass stupidity?

Dylan

The relief that you feel, once you're alone again in the hollow, gives a clue to the extent of your surrender. Under the spell cast by the fleeting smile of the stranger for whom you now wait, you've dared to think again about love after a broken love. What must you have read into that smile in the hours since your meeting that has so besotted you? Are you making a complete fool of yourself? But when Eurig greets you with the most chaste of kisses on the cheek, you know these are the wrong questions.

They talked as they walked along the beach towards the island where Llanddwyn's chaste isolation was held hostage by the low tide. Neither noticed the nude bathers that marked the transition from the gayer end nearer the point, nor the cute daddies — with their bikinied women and sunburnt children to protect them — who tended not to stray much beyond the forest boundary in the middle of Llanddwyn Bay. Immersed in one another's intimacy, Eurig and Dylan revealed the bits of their lives they hoped the other would find relevant and engaging. Bound by the charmed circles that each had cast around the other, both dared to believe they'd discover the meeting points that might hold them together and give a context to the carnality each now knew they would share.

Sitting on lichen covered stones that might once have been part of Dwynwen's convent on the island, Eurig told Dylan how, in the fifth century, King Brychan's daughter suffered for love and had then, much later, become the patron saint of Welsh lovers. With a cheeky smile, Dylan said that they'd better steer clear of syrupy drinks in case their hearts turned cold like Dwynwen's, or worse still, they both turned into ice like Maelon, her lover. Then

Eurig led Dylan to Dwynwen's well, where legend had it that the fate of lovers could be determined in the movements of the fish that swam there. Dylan laughed when he saw the shallow, miry puddle and with an exaggerated sigh at the prospect of doomed fortune he said that the fish obviously didn't dance for the likes of them. Eurig waved his hands over the murky pit like a crazed, camp old witch, calling on the fish to reveal their secrets. Bending low over Dwynwen's well he caught the glint of something brilliant in the mud.

From the rock that had split so the dying Dwynwen could recline and bask in her last sunset, Dylan and Eurig watched the sky turn red and they thought up fables about the gold gimmal ring. The mud had come away easily enough from the ring's interlocking hands, and the heart that the fingers embraced had retained its lustre. Lost or thrown aside? Some careless lapse or the vengeful and deliberate action of an angry lover? Or perhaps the fish were telling them something after all? Then Dylan kissed Eurig deeply. Their senses sated with sensual pleasures and sex almost took them over. Eurig drew away, fearing that this exquisite promise might be washed away by grief and loss.

The tide rolled in over Malltraeth Bay's wide sands and the waves restored to Dwynwen a fragile virginity. The sun set, and they sat in silence, high up on the deserted beach, both hoping for a new beginning and wondering if they dared entrust it to the other. And when sex's possibility made their talking futile, they swam, confident that the effort would tire them and the cold numb their mutual desire. Later, wrapped in one another's tired arms at the sea's edge, where dying waves lapped their vulnerability, Eurig yielded to the whispered promise and the rhythm of Dylan's body.

Dylan

The familiar path in the firebreak through the Corsican pines, which down the years has always seemed endless, brings you all too quickly to the clearing where you've left your car. You want to accept Eurig's invitation to rest for the few hours that remain of the night, but you recognise that the odds are against there being much calm between you. You need at least a few hours sleep if you're to make it through the morning clinic. And you want some time by yourself to question your motives and consider the fishes' prophecy.

Eurig

Already missing Dylan, you lay on the chaise-longue and stare at the red light on the new answering machine, almost as though to de-code its Morse-like flashes. You are half afraid to listen to whatever voice has been recorded, in case its message pulls you back into the debris of your broken family. Eventually you hear Seimon say that he's sorry; he asks if you can meet. Through Fflur's window, the dawn bloodies the sky over Snowdonia. You tug the chaise across the living room, dragging the rug with it. Lying in its familiar embrace, grateful that you no longer have to watch the comings and goings of the men along the path just beyond the buddleia bush, you roll Dwynwen's gimmal ring in your fingers. When Dylan comes to you, you slip it onto his little finger and swim with him in the dawn.

A Particular Passion

Over lunch, which they ate in the spring sunshine outside the Education Authority training centre, Ben Pasgen and his two colleagues wondered if either of the workshop facilitators had ever stood in front of a class of fourteen-year-olds; the theories they expounded seemed so untouched by practice.

"It's all very well saying we should question our motives for being involved in sex education," Gwern said. A newly qualified teacher in his first job, his speech was instantly recognisable as Cardiganshire Welsh. He continued, "I was just told that it was a part of the tutorial class-work and that I might get to go on a course if there's some spare cash at the end of the year. I don't have a motive for my involvement: I just feel coerced." Catrin, the head of RE from the largest school in the area, said that since the Assembly's new Sex Education guidelines had come in they'd had to involve reluctant teachers who'd had no specialised training too, but at least their school policy was quite clear about what could and could not be taught; "Our biggest problem as a group of staff," she explained, "is dealing with personal questions and disclosures. I know that kids can play up and they often just ask things to test you, or see if they can embarrass you, but sometimes you get the sense that a question is genuine. Just recently some of the girls in Year Eleven asked if I'd had sex before I was married."

"What did you say?" Ben quizzed.

"I asked them why they wanted to know," Catrin said straightforwardly. "It's a good tactic with personal questions, it gives you a bit of time to think and it helps you judge if they're trying it on."

"And what did they say?" asked Gwern.

"Well, one of the girls said she was feeling pressured by her boyfriend and another, who'd thought she was ready, had carted her boyfriend off to see the Family Planning people and they'd both come away feeling a bit unsure. They were talking so sensibly, and they wanted to know how I'd dealt with my first sexual experiences."

"So how much of yourself do you give away, Catrin?" Ben asked, searching her face with his grey eyes.

"That's a hard one," she said with a shrug. "It all depends on what sort of life you've led, I suppose. I've only ever slept with one man and we did sleep together before we were married, but I was twenty-two and engaged and we kept having to put the wedding off because Paul's mother had cancer. I didn't mind sharing that with the girls… but perhaps if I'd had sex with two or three boyfriends when I was in college, or if I'd had an abortion at 15, or maybe if I was a lesbian, I might not have wanted to say too much. Kids can be bloody cruel if they think they've got something on you."

Ben lay on the top bench, his head cradled in his hands; he felt the sweat trickle into his armpits. Except for the second Friday of the month, his slot on the duty rota of the gay line in Bangor, he spent every Friday evening at The Steamworks. The by-pass around Y Felinheli and the ludicrously fast A55 meant that he could get there from his remote hillside cottage in just over an hour. As the sauna's heat eased the tightness of the knots in his shoulders and soothed the pain of his rheumaticky hands, his preoccupation with the sex education workshop earlier that day, and Catrin's comments about answering personal questions, gave way to thoughts of sexual desire and gratification.

Some of the regulars were already there: Tony, the boy from "parks and gardens", Gwyn and Iolo, the vicar and the GP who always came together, Eddy, who taught at the university in Bangor and Stan, the chip shop owner from Llandudno. Ben didn't knowingly have sex with any of this group, though in the steam room it wasn't always easy to know who was who; these were the men he sat around with and talked to about politics and travel, gardening and DIY. It was still early, but there were a couple of strangers that excited him; this was how Ben had grown to like it — anonymous sex was so uncomplicated. This way he could be certain, when he left The Steamworks, that no one would be likely to turn up on his door step or phone him at school... and he could be sure that he wouldn't become emotionally involved.

It wasn't that somewhere deep inside him he didn't yearn for one man to love and share his life with. A long time ago, nearly sixteen years, he'd made a choice to return to Gwynedd and immerse himself in Welsh life. Though Manchester had seemed tempting, since the gay scene had come into its own, offering freedoms and choices that would be out of reach in Meirionnydd, the chance to teach science in a new Welsh-medium school and to live his everyday life in his mother tongue touched him at his identity's core. He knew well enough that such a choice would demand that his gayness remain in the closet, but Ben Pasgen was neither disappointed nor dissatisfied with his life. Just like the peppered moth, the example he always cited to his GCSE class when explaining the theory of natural selection, he had adapted successfully to a potentially hostile environment.

Ben's experience of sex in The Steamworks was often bizarre, but it was always safe: it was as though the group voiced a silent message about self-preservation that no one transgressed. One of the staff replenished the supplies of condoms and lubricating gel once or twice through the course of an evening; like fruit or sweets, they lay in bowls on occasional tables for customers to help themselves. It was with some pride that Ben would occasionally reflect on the fact that for all his brief encounters, with perhaps fifty, seventy, even a hundred men a year, he'd never caught an infection. But then he wasn't complacent either, and knowing that some STIs developed no symptoms, he had himself checked over at the clinic in Wrexham every school holiday. Since the cute new consultant had arrived, Ben almost looked forward to these visits.

His colleagues at school, the faithful few on the Parochial Church Council and the dwindling congregation at Eglwys Sant Pedr, his co-campaigners in Plaid Cymru and his friends in the choir would have been shocked and scandalised had they known of Ben's evenings at The Steamworks. Some, he felt sure, would be disgusted and want no more to do with him. Yet, he'd always been careful not to deliberately mislead people or lie to them, and in all the years he'd been back in Wales, no one had asked about his "private life". Perhaps the visible busyness of his days precluded, in most people's minds, any notion of his having a private life. But he knew well enough how people made assumptions about others... how they filled in the gaps of other people's lives with their own fancies and fictions. Ben couldn't know the untruths in which they'd clothed him.

For some weeks after the sex education workshop, when he was driving or in the middle of some renovation job on his cottage, Ben had thought about how he might respond if a student asked him about his sex life. He'd tried rehearsing different scenarios and anticipating responses, but gay and lesbian issues were not part of everyday conversation in the cafés of Dolgellau, the pubs of Trawsfynydd or the staff room at Ysgol Bro Meirion, so the imaginary role-play only led to an uneasy paranoia. He liked the idea of establishing a "no personal questions" ground rule with his classes, but he also liked Catrin's suggestion: "Ask them why they want to know". He couldn't help wondering how many boys and girls, in his fifteen years at Bro Meirion, had been confused and tormented by the realisation that they were gay or lesbian and found no information or support at school. He remembered the fear and loneliness of his own school days. Ask them why they want to know, he repeated to himself.

When the question came it wasn't during a sex education lesson. This might have thrown Ben, had gay sex not surfaced again on all the front pages in connection with political sleaze and subconsciously prepared him. He'd encouraged the students in Wednesday's Year Ten tutor group to bring in cuttings from newspapers and magazines for comment and debate. Iddon, the brawny tight-head prop who secretly worried that he was the only virgin in the scrum, began the discussion.

"What about all these homos in Parliament, then?" he asked the class, holding up the front page of a tabloid with the headline *Queer Goings-on in the House*. A clutch of Iddon's gang began to giggle. Ben ignored them and addressed the class:

"Okay... this story's been running for a couple of days now. Has anyone else been following it?"

Manon put up her hand and said, "That's the story I've brought in too, Sir..." and with a trace of scorn in her voice she continued, "but my cutting is from *The Independent*."

"Good, Manon," Ben smiled. "And anyone else? Hands up all of you who know something about this."

Most of the class put up their hands.

"All right then," Ben said, sitting on the table at the front of the class, "why don't we ask Iddon and Manon to give a brief summary of how the two different newspapers have reported this story... and perhaps both of you would like to tell us what you think about it before we open up to the class. Okay? Iddon, why don't you start?"

"Sir, this story's about two MPs. They're both married men with kids," Iddon lifted his right arm and dangled his wrist limply, "but they've been having it off with other men."

Some of his pack made cringing faces and grunting noises; signs of their disgust, Ben wondered, or just their own adolescent insecurity? Iddon continued, "I think the main point in this article is that men like these shouldn't be trusted. They shouldn't be allowed to be MPs... and... well, Sir, I think they should all be put on an island and have their balls cut off."

Iddon's supporters cheered and clapped.

"Thank you for that, Iddon," Ben said, with a smile, anticipating the lively responses his proposed treatment for gay men might evoke. "That's enough cheers or we'll have complaints from next door. Come on then, Manon, let's hear what you've got to say."

She stood up and took a deep breath, as if trying to swell her tiny body to gain some authority: "The main argument of this article," she said with all the confidence of a regular eisteddfod winner in recitation and public speaking, "is that for as long as our society remains intolerant of homosexuals and lesbians, and is reluctant to see them taking prominent positions in our public life, there will be men and women who will feel forced to lead double lives, a public life which seems to conform to society's expectations and a private life which is secret and furtive. And of course, if people feel they've got something to conceal, then they will hide behind lies and deception and so their integrity is called into question." She looked around the class and wondered if her points had been put clearly enough. "Personally," she pushed a strand of hair back behind her ear, "I feel very sorry for these two Members of Parliament, not because I approve of the way they've treated their families or misled their constituents, but because they have not felt able to be themselves. I'm sorry for them because they've had to live a lie and I would hope that our generation," she paused and looked at Iddon and his supporters, "I would hope that our generation will work to eliminate discrimination against homosexuals and be open to understanding their lifestyle. I see no reason, in the future, why we shouldn't have a lesbian leader of Plaid Cymru or why there shouldn't be a gay night at the Deri Arms in *Pobol y Cwm*. I don't understand why people are frightened and threatened by homosexuals, but I think the key to lifting the threat and easing the fear is better education."

In the silence that gripped the class, Manon sat down triumphantly; even Iddon seemed to be held in the transient embrace of her challenge.

The class debate was slow to kindle. Iddon's ideas seemed too extreme for the majority, and were, anyway, quite impractical. Which island would they choose and wouldn't homosexuals hide if they knew they were going to be castrated? But Manon was accused of being too liberal; she hadn't considered the immorality of homosexuality or the corrupting influence people like that had on young people and on family life. And then Richard, one of Iddon's rugby mates, asked, "Do you know any queers then, Sir?"

"Yes, a few," Ben replied.

Iddon, rocking on his chair, asked cockily, "You one then, Sir?"

"That's a very personal question, Iddon," Ben responded with no trace of hesitation. "Why would you want to know?"

"So that I can keep my back to the wall, Sir," Iddon fired straight back.

His cronies laughed. Ben felt sick inside, but his face remained calm and in the second he gave to his thoughts, Miriam came back at Iddon, "And what makes you think that Sir would even fancy you?"

The class's laughter cut her off and Iddon turned redder than a Comic Relief plastic nose.

"Well, thank you Miriam," Ben said, trying to lighten the heaviness that pressed on him. "You credit me with more taste than that, then?"

"Oh — he makes me sick, Sir," Miriam said mockingly. "He thinks he's sex on a stick."

"That's enough, Miriam," Ben said. "I think Iddon is embarrassed enough, don't make it worse for him."

"Yeah — well, Sir..." Miriam smiled at Ben. She liked him.

Tracy, one of the brassiest girls in the class, called from across the room, "If you were gay then, Sir, who would you fancy?"

"Why would you want to know if I'm gay, Tracy?"

"Well," she shrugged, "then we could talk about men, Sir, you know, compare notes. What do you think about Robson

Green or that gorgeous Michael Owen?"

"No, Tracy," Ben said, shaking his head and smiling broadly. "I don't think I'll be joining you in the girls' toilet to do make-up and talk about boys." And addressing the class through their laughter, he continued, "All right, let's try and pull the threads of this debate together and see what we're left with."

After Ben had summarised their discussion and highlighted some of the sticking points he felt they ought to think about, Manon put her hand up: "Mr Pasgen, you also left us with a question. You asked us why we would want to know if you are gay? You haven't actually said that you are gay... but you haven't said that you're not either." She seemed to be judging essence and detail as she spoke. "I think that the uncertainty you've left us with would be a really good thing for us to consider. I mean, if you, or any of our teachers at Bro Meirion are gay, does it make any difference to us in this class, to our parents, or to other kids and teachers in school?"

"Well done, Manon," Ben said, his heart pounding so thunderously he wondered if those closest to him could hear it. "I think that would be a good exercise to do during the week. It'll get us all thinking about our prejudices and our willingness — or unwillingness — to be tolerant and understanding. Good.... Thank you... all of you who contributed. We can come back to this discussion next week."

The students erupted into exchanges around the room, which only the bell interrupted. As Ben dismissed the class the knotted muscles that had cramped his stomach and constricted his shoulders began to slacken and the rhythm of his heart regained its imperceptible certainty.

Miss Edwards the school secretary came to the junior science laboratory towards the end of the afternoon while Ben was teaching. She handed him a note from Mr Hopcyn, the headteacher: he needed to see Ben immediately after the bell. Ifan Hopcyn's straight-talking brusqueness had upset a number of the staff in the two years he'd been at Bro Meirion, but Ben could only speak as he found, and he liked him. As the children cleared away their things, Ben wondered if the Head had finally got a decision for him on the Year Twelve field trip.

Ben heard Catrin's advice echo in his mind and without flinching he looked into Ifan Hopcyn's grey eyes and asked, "Why do you want to know if I'm a homosexual?"

"I've got the reputation of a school to defend and over three hundred adolescent boys to protect," he said, almost pleading. "Don't you think that those are good enough reasons for me to know?"

"But I'm not clear why the school's reputation needs to be defended nor what the boys need protecting from," Ben replied firmly.

"I've heard that you told your Year Ten tutor group you might be a homosexual."

"No," Ben interrupted. "We had a discussion about homosexuality which Iddon Jones and your daughter, Manon, introduced with clippings from today's newspapers."

Ben recounted the direction of the arguments and explained how, when asked if he was gay, he'd deliberately chosen to be ambiguous so that the class would think about the issue in general terms and not get caught up in personalities.

"But I still need to know, Ben," Ifan Hopcyn said. "When parents start phoning me up worried about their children's physical and moral welfare I have to be able to put their minds at rest either by telling them that you're not a homosexual, or if you are, that I've taken all the necessary steps..."

"What are you talking about, Mr Hopcyn?" Ben asked, with an edge of disbelief in his tone. "We're at the end of the twentieth century now... not the nineteenth!"

"People in this community will not tolerate a homosexual teaching their children, damn it!" Ifan Hopcyn banged his desk with a solid fist. "We're not living in a left-wing London borough, Ben — this is *cefn gwlad* for God's sake," he said, his voice raised.

A terse silence overwhelmed them.

When Ifan Hopcyn spoke again he'd regained his composure, "I won't have homosexuals teaching at this school and I believe that the governors will support me in this."

"You're going to put every teacher at Bro Meirion through this then," Ben said. "Some kind of purge, to cull the so-called morally unacceptable?"

"Is that your admission?" he asked.

Ben shook his head and smiling wryly he said, "No... no, it's not an admission of anything. My answer to your question about whether I'm gay is the same as I gave to Year Ten this morning."

"I'm sorry that you've chosen to be so unco-operative and unprofessional, Ben," he said, strumming his fingers on his desk. "I'll talk with as many of the governors as I can this afternoon and this evening; don't be surprised if you're suspended until I can call a full meeting of the board."

Ben sighed and shook his head in utter disbelief. As he got up to leave he said quietly and with as much dignity as he could grasp, "If your bigotry, Ifan Hopcyn, extends to the board of governors, then my days at Bro Meirion are surely numbered, so let me say this. I've given fifteen years of my working life to build the academic reputation of the science department in this school, and I've worked pretty damn hard to turn out some decent, well-rounded young people. Consider me unco-operative if you will, but don't ever call my professionalism as a teacher into question. If I am a gay man then think about this. Being gay wouldn't be something that got switched on like a light this morning. Fifteen years suggest that it is not my suitability as a teacher that's at issue here. Something far bigger is at stake."

"Child protection is what's at issue here, Ben," Ifan Hopcyn spat out. "Like every parent of a child in this school, I'm concerned that no vulnerable boys are buggered by a sodomite."

Ben was silenced by the affront of the Head Teacher's allusion. Closing the door of the office behind him a pain in the palm of his right hand made him wince.

Ben keyed into the memory of the CD player the track

numbers of the opera's overture and Rienzi's aria from the beginning of act five. They played alternately at full volume, for there were no neighbours on Ben's hillside to be disturbed. He watched the colours of the sunset play on the river far below and the menacing clouds swirl around the giant's throne high across the valley. Wagner's music invaded the remotest recesses of Ben's consciousness, its turbulence routing the recollected insults, its tenderness pacifying his spirit.

The red flashes of the answering machine bore witness to the calls that the music had muted. Ben listened first to Gomer Prys, choir leader and governor at Bro Meirion: "...given your trouble it would be better if you don't sing at the Easter concerts." Then Ieuan from the local Plaid campaign team, also on the governing board: "Hopcyn's got it all wrong, of course; I have told him, Ben. The stupid bugger thinks all gays are paedophiles... but then, you know, perhaps a lot of the locals will think that too... so, maybe, with this hanging over you, like, it won't do the election campaign any good to have you out canvassing. Sorry Ben." And Ifan Hopcyn: "...I've talked with seven of the governors and the unanimous feeling was that we call an emergency meeting next week. Until then you're suspended. Do not come to school until further notice. I'll put all this in writing for you." The same stabbing pain that had earlier caused his right hand to clench now contorted the left one.

In the minutes before the morning assembly, Manon, who'd heard enough from her father's study to know what was going on, persuaded four of her friends that it was the right thing to do. They had to stand against bigotry and injustice. When everyone else sat down after singing the hymn, the five remained standing. Manon, in her clearest eisteddfod voice, announced that she thought she might be a lesbian and wondered when she could expect to be suspended like Mr Pasgen. None of her four friends let her down, each voice rising above the commotion that was breaking out in the school hall:

"I think I'm a lesbian too...."

"I think I may be gay...."

Ifan Hopcyn called for silence and for a moment the hall became quiet. Then, to Manon's surprise, Tracy stood up in the row before them:

"It doesn't matter if Mr Pasgen is gay, he's the best teacher we've got," she said, her voice faltering, betraying a softer, more vulnerable quality that surprised many in the assembly. And a cheer grew louder through the hall and more students rose to their feet. Mr Hopcyn's face went from red to purple. Though he called out for order, more than a third of the gathered students stood in defiance of his authority.

Ben knew nothing of the minor insurrection unfolding at Bro Meirion that Thursday morning; nor did he know that by the final bell of the afternoon, Manon and Tracy's unlikely alliance had given birth to a petition in his support, which had been signed by over four hundred of the school's six hundred pupils. Ben had thought he would spend the morning on the phone getting some advice from the teaching unions, but the morning sunshine was warm, so he sat in his garden and watched the insects dip into the blood red of the tulips cascading over the steep terraces. He rubbed balm into his palms and knuckles but the pain gnawed deeply. Through the open windows, resounding across the valley to the majestic Cader where Ben sometimes imagined God to be seated, Wagner's music soared and Rienzi's plea, *Almighty Father, look down upon me...* echoed Ben's own prayer. A prayer from another hillside in another time.

The Wedding Invitation

Just after the Penyffordd by-pass, Seth always begins to feel that Wales really is his home. He'll never belong in Liverpool even though the city has, for more than a decade, breathed into him the courage to become himself. As the dual carriageways of the Wirral and Deeside yield to the country roads that snake through the Clwydian range, the hills, with their lush, deep purples and greens of late spring, embrace Seth in a welcome home. Freddy Mercury's lament, The Great Pretender, bawling from the speakers on auto-repeat since driving into the Mersey Tunnel, jars with the mood of belonging that grips him. Ejecting Freddy, he pushes Leah Owen into the gaping mouth of the cassette player, the tape that had made him so homesick during that year in Israel with Jude.

Bala, for as long as he can remember, is the place where the journey from Liverpool to home has always been broken: for a pee, for chips, to buy a loaf of bread from the bakery that Seth's father is almost willing to admit bakes finer bread than he himself bakes in the Williams Family Bakery. In honour of this tradition Seth stops for ten minutes. He walks up the High Street as far as the Welsh Craft Shop to look at the Welsh wool sweaters rich in blues, reds and greens... and to finger the smoothness of a love spoon, before returning to the car and continuing the journey.

Passing the lake, just minutes west of Bala, Seth remembers a day spent walking in the hills around Llyn Tegid with the Liverpool University Ramblers' Club. He hadn't known Jude well then, but they'd both talked a lot that day; mostly about Jude's interest in uncovering the story of a whole branch of his family that was gassed and burnt in the ovens at Auschwitz. He'd been fascinated by Jude, but had found him frightening too. Three years older, he'd talked about how learning of the fate of his family in that Polish death camp had woken him up to the Nazi persecution of gays during the years of the Third Reich, and how this forgotten history had become the focus of his doctoral thesis. That had been in '86 or '87, before Seth had woken up to himself. His sense of identity then had lacked honesty or integrity, and he'd found such talk painful.

Jude hadn't been invited to Seth's sister Naomi's wedding. Seth cast his mind back to their breakfast, earlier that Friday morning.

"You can't disappoint your sister, Seth," he'd urged. "You can't just decide not to go."

The arguments around why Jude was being excluded had been almost exhausted over the past weeks. Seth had hated being the messenger, especially when that had involved reminding Jude of his mother Ceinwen's particular animosity.

"'A traditional family wedding in the countryside, at the Welsh heartland; that's no place for the two of you to be seen together,'" Seth had mimicked Ceinwen's rising pitch. "'And it's not right anyway that a man should keep such close company with another man! People in the village will talk! Not to mention that this other man is a Jew...'" They'd both been able to laugh at Ceinwen's histrionics. "But then she always backtracks too," Seth went on, "pretending she's got your interests at heart and worrying that you'd feel left out with everyone speaking Welsh!"

"That's a joke!" Jude had exploded. "Has she forgotten that Chris — the groom, for God's sake — is a Bristol man who talks like he's got Victoria plums in his mouth?"

But their roles had been cast, and over their coffee that morning the hurt, but understanding lover had persuaded Seth that he should attend the wedding alone.

The recollection of Jude speaking his pain that morning reopens the wound of Seth's parents' denial and rejection. It smarts deeply, triggering a yearning to hold Jude, and be held by him. He pulls over into a lay-by at the side of the lake, and at the water's edge wills the beauty of the afternoon to calm the emotional cross-currents coursing through him: love for Jude pulling against the loyalty he believes is owed to sister and parents. For seven years and three months he's shared a love with Jude that neither of them had ever believed might be possible. Since they've known about them as a couple, Seth's parents have denied the reality of his happiness with Jude. Ceinwen, from the beginning, has only ever referred to him as *that Jewish man*. As the storm rages, Seth wishes that his parents could take a leaf from Jude's mother and father.

The Canters hadn't actually welcomed Seth with open arms either; they too had found it hard to accept that their son loved another man. But, with time, they'd softened: Nina Canter had even bought Seth a boxed set of Edith Piaf CDs one birthday after hearing that Piaf's passion moved him to tears.

Back in the car, fingering the steering wheel in hesitation, Seth pictures the uproar that the phone call he wants to make will create: *Dwi'n aros yn Lerpwl efo Jude....* He imagines how Ceinwen, on hearing his refusal, will be even more hostile towards Jude. She'll go on about how he can't show greater loyalty to that Jew than to his own family: "You have to come to the wedding... you can't stay in Liverpool — not this weekend."

And he pictures Jude, more dear to him than anyone in the world, and remembers how reasonable he's been through the whole messy affair.

With Piaf at full volume Seth continues west. After Dolgellau he winds the car with the Mawddach to the wide estuary and the coast. The village signpost still bears the scars of the fatal accident more than a year ago, one of its poles rusted and bent, the bold lettering pitched at sixty degrees. Not much seems to have changed in the village. Before reaching the house he passes the bakery: the sign, *M. Z. Williams & Son — Fine Bakers... Baking your Daily*

Bread since 1922 has been repainted. Miss Morris, who's worked for his father for half a lifetime, is standing at the door talking to Mrs Caradog the Minister's wife... about their rig-outs for the wedding, most likely. Mrs Caradog will be exasperated, as is her way, by the prices of everything in Chester... she always shops in Chester, Browns, so dependable! Miss Morris will be retelling, in every detail, how Nancy Parry helped her choose from the lovely selection of twin sets in stock at London House... new for the spring and very reasonable. Miss Morris recognises Seth and waves a welcome, which he returns. At the village's only traffic light he turns right into Enlli View Road. The Llyn Peninsula and Bardsey Island fill the windscreen after the turn. The signpost still shows stains from a dousing with green paint. The Language Campaign seems years ago now.

By dinnertime that evening Ceinwen Williams had re-ironed her son's shirt, sponged and pressed his suit and expressed her distaste for the tie he'd chosen to wear. Seth cares little for his mother's taste in ties and is actually grateful that she'd troubled with his suit... but Jude had ironed his shirt that morning and her re-ironing of it was an interference that he resents. He hadn't expected to be alone with his mother. Naomi had been home most of the week and he'd assumed that she would be about, fussing. But Seth had caught only the briefest glimpse of his sister. Her best friend from school and now her bridesmaid-to-be, Shân, had phoned as Seth had walked in through the door to say that her car had broken down the other side of Dinas Mawddwy. Naomi had rushed to rescue Shân, while Chris was checking that his family were all settled at the George III Hotel in Penmaen Pool.

Stirring the gravy, just Seth and his mother in the kitchen, he ventures to share his most recent good news: that from September Jude will be Senior Lecturer in Modern History at Liverpool University. Ceinwen straightens her back as she lays the masher on the worktop beside the steaming pan of mashed potato. She spits the words out in her precise Caernarfonshire Welsh: "That Jewish

man's success is none of my concern. It's time you settled down...
properly! Family weddings are not the time to bring disgrace on us."

Still stirring the gravy, and not looking at her, Seth talks about
how much he loves Jude; how it's a creative and whole and special
and wonderful relationship... and that they're both very happy
together. Surely that's what's important... to have found happiness
and not be a lonely, twisted, insecure, frightened person? But before
all the words are spoken, Chris and Naomi burst into the kitchen.
Ceinwen's eyes catch Seth's for a fleeting second, pleading — and
demanding at the same time — that no more be said.

The family gathers around the table to eat. Ceinwen had
decided it would be convenient to all concerned that the five of
them should eat at home, and then go over to the George III after
Chris's family had rested and eaten. Seth is struck by the
strangeness of English conversation around the dining table of his
family home. His mother speaks English with an affected twang.
His father's grasp of the language is laboured and makes him
sound a bit stupid, which he isn't. Naomi's Welsh accent, however,
is scarcely audible.

The wedding talk gives way to disconnected snippets from
work, respective family histories, last year's holidays, the new
ovens in the bakery and the price of Welsh lamb, which Ceinwen
believes to be robbery, but then Welsh is so much tastier than New
Zealand! And then Chris asks Seth how Jude is.

Seth smiles at him and fleetingly wonders whether his
question is born of naivety or rebellion. He shares the news of
Jude's success in getting the Senior Lectureship.

"Well done, Jude!" murmurs Chris, adding, "It's a shame he
can't be with you this time."

Seth's father Mostyn stops eating, his fork poised, his eyes
fixed on the remains of the Welsh lamb's leg. Ceinwen has flushed,
her face as crimson as her frock, her stare intent on silencing Chris.
He seems oblivious, confident even that he'll be his own man, son-
in-law to the imperious Ceinwen or no.

"Has Jude's thesis been published yet?" he asks. Ceinwen's

rudeness reveals how flagrant she finds Chris's disregard for her version of the family code. Addressing Naomi directly in Welsh she snaps, "Chris must understand that Seth's misadventure with that Jewish man is not acceptable family conversation."

"If you want to say something to Chris," Naomi answers in English, "you'd better speak to him in a language that he can understand!"

Mostyn lays his fork on his plate, and takes Ceinwen's shaking hand on the table.

"Our background and generation," he murmurs to Chris with profound humility, "make it difficult to accept Seth's choices in life. We would rather you spared us the embarrassment."

The dining room falls silent but as the seconds slip away the chink of knives and forks fills the quiet that had separated the family.

Chris is offered more lamb, which he declines. Ceinwen's interpretation of his refusal is explained to the gathering... that he's saving room for her *tarten 'fale*. On some previous visit Chris had raved about Ceinwen's apple tart, which had thrilled her no end and scored him lots of points, and he'd eaten three huge slices at a single sitting. On every subsequent visit Chris had been served Ceinwen's *tarten 'fale* for dessert. As she rises from the table she turns to Naomi requesting her help in the kitchen.

As though Seth were invisible, Mostyn says to Chris, almost by way of apology, "Ceinwen really can't cope at all with Seth being one of the sons of Sodom."

Chris, moving closer to Seth and putting his arm around his shoulder, shakes his head and replies, "To deny Jude's existence is sad. As Seth's brother-in-law I'll respect his integrity. I won't become part of your denial, Mostyn!"

Mostyn's face softens and, nodding his head slowly, he answers, "Perhaps that's how it should be in these modern times. Ceinwen and I haven't experienced city life; in our *milltir sgwâr*..." Breaking off, he searches for the English idiom and then, with a prompt from Seth continues, "In our square mile of life such a thing is sinful and unnatural, bringing diseases and disgrace." Silence falls over the table again.

Seth feels like hugging them both for their honesty but is prevented by uncertainty from even speaking. His father's pain is so real, and as much as he wants to acknowledge it, Seth doesn't want him to think that he accepts even a hair's breadth of his position. Chris, in a gesture that further emphasises his support for Seth, draws him closer until their heads touch and, almost in a private whisper, asks, "When are you and Jude coming to visit us in Bristol?"

For a moment, before Seth mouths the words accepting Chris' invitation, he sees the agony tearing through his father's face and he knows that he'll never come home again.

As Seth and Chris begin to talk about the things they might all do in Bristol, Mostyn excuses himself, explaining that he needs to check that everything is ready for later that evening when, alone in the bakery, he'll bake bread for the village through the night. "But I'll need help with the apple tart," Chris jokingly protests.

Mostyn forces a laugh and leaves them.

"I really appreciate you standing with me, Chris," Seth thanks him.

After eating too much apple tart, Seth and Chris offer to wash up the dinner dishes, so the two women disappear to make themselves ready for the get-together at the pub. Mostyn turns up in the kitchen, dressed and ready to go, just in time to put the dried dishes away.

The spring breeze blowing up the Mawddach from Cardigan Bay, seven miles away, has soured the promise of a mild evening. The George III at Penmaen Pool on the estuary echoes with Bristolian accents, all the rooms having been booked by Chris' family and friends months in advance. After ten minutes Seth begins to feel out of place. These are Chris and Naomi's family, not mine, he thinks. With a deepening anxiety about his need to censor whatever he might say, in case he causes some upset, Seth begins to wish he'd stayed home in the village. Regretting that he hadn't come in his own car he begins to feel trapped. He looks into his pint of Guinness... out at the river... thinks about Jude... looks into his pint again. Then Chris breaks into Seth's longing to leave and introduces his best man, Robert.

Alone together at a window overlooking the toll bridge that crosses the river, Seth and Robert become instantly easy with one another. Seth can't work out why neither Chris nor his sister have ever mentioned Robert before.

"Call me Robby," he says, and before long they've progressed to scoring the two barmen. "I reckon they're both trade, what d'you think?"

"Maybe... I hadn't given it much thought," Seth responds with a coy smile.

"You can have the one with curly hair," Robby gestures with a wink. "I've only scored him a seven on the bed-able scale. Now that dark rugby player type... he gets a nine in my book!"

Not being that interested in scoring with either of the barmen, Seth asks him, "How do you know Chris and Naomi?" Robby's life history spans the next half hour and another pint of Guinness.

While Robby's taking a pee Seth realises that he's cheered up. The alcohol has eased the tension that had tied knots across his shoulders as the day wore on, and meeting Robby has made him feel less a stranger in his own land. He watches the cars as they drive parallel to the river's edge and turn to cross the toll bridge, their headlights catching the bats in flight. He loves this river and its valley; he knows every mile of it from cycle rides, walks and childhood explorations, from the wide estuary with its railway bridge at Barmouth to its trickling source in the wild hills of Meirionnydd above Coed y Brenin. He remembers expeditions to the Clogau and Gwynfynydd gold mines and the adventures.... Robby returns, all smiles: "The bar man's name is something unpronounceable in Welsh — no vowels! He does play rugby and he lives in. We're meeting up later on. Wish me luck!"

Much later, Seth is sitting at the kitchen table with Naomi.

Sharing what's left of the *tarten 'fale*, and drinking cups of tea, she talks about the old friends she's met again that evening, while Seth listens. She talks about Chris' family and tries to make the family connections for him. Then Seth chats about Robby and she can't believe that he's got a date with the bar man.

"Are you happy?" Seth asks. She replies, nodding, "*Hapus iawn.*"

The kitchen door opens and Ceinwen joins them. Naomi reaches for a mug and pours her some tea.

"Are you all ready for tomorrow?" she asks Naomi, who nods. "We're proud that you're marrying so well even though we were disappointed when you first announced the engagement," Ceinwen ventured once again onto dangerous ground, "marrying into an English family and all... I'll have to speak with my grandchildren in a foreign language."

"*Paid a dechra Mam, nid heno,*" Naomi warns. "Don't let's go over this again, it's all been said before, not tonight of all nights."

Seth breaks in, asking his mother why she finds it so hard to accept that her children are making the choices that are right for them... and not for her... not for other people. Naomi bangs her mug on the table, "*Paid ti a dechra chwaith, Seth,*" she points with her finger, don't you start either!

Seth gets up from the table, kisses Naomi on the cheek and goes to leave the kitchen.

"*Oes gen ti un i dy fam hefyd?*" Ceinwen wants him to kiss her too.

He turns at the door: "No I haven't got a kiss for you. I won't play by your rules any more. If it's your choice to deny me, and the people and relationships that are important to me... if it's your choice to be so rude as to call Jude *that Jewish man* all the time..." Seth is gathering steam now. "If you can't accept me and my choices then it would be better if I didn't come home again. There... I've said it." Seth closes the kitchen door behind him.

From the bedroom window Seth can see the lights of

Barmouth across the wide estuary mouth where the waters of the Mawddach join the bay. In the far distance the shimmer of Pwllheli's lights seem to dance with the stars on the low horizon. He grew up with the view from this window. He knows its moods... wild at times, ever changing, always beautiful. Its familiarity is a comfort to the finality of his words: *It will be better if I don't come home again.*

Beginning to undress, the thought strikes Seth that at this time of night he can be back home in Liverpool in just two hours. He thinks about the three pints of Guinness and then about Naomi. Having removed all his clothes, he slips naked between the fresh cotton sheets and tries to conjure the warmth and presence of Jude's body next to him. In Jude's arms, in the absolute knowledge and confidence of their love for one another, sleep comes easily.

Walking the few hundred yards to the chapel, Seth reflects on the rightness of his decision not to flee back to Liverpool in the small hours. Rising early, he had walked a couple of miles through the village and its immediate surroundings, along the beach and up into the centre of the ancient stone circle in Cae Cynhaeaf, the field behind the parish church, where he'd said goodbye to his home patch. Back at the house by eight thirty, little was said at the breakfast table, indeed, he'd been left with a pot of coffee and the local paper. Children from the village still gather at the chapel gates, just like he and Naomi had done when they were children. The kids distract him... bring him from his thoughts to face Robby, standing at the doors of the chapel with an usher, smiling mischievously as he climbs the steps.

Naomi looks beautiful. Seth is surprised that she must have won the battle against tradition, since she is walking down the aisle between her parents. Ceinwen looks elegant, but then this is the occasion on which she has to out-do Mrs Caradog the Minister's wife, who, in Seth's judgement has chosen the wrong colour. Miss Morris hasn't been let down by the new spring collection in London House. The Bristol set look city sophisticated, like a troupe of extras from the set of an American soap opera. Robby looks so stunningly handsome Seth gets an erection. Mr Caradog handles the bi-lingual service well; Naomi says her vows in Welsh, Chris speaks his in English. It's a simple, dignified ceremony, and most importantly, Mr Caradog keeps his Welsh orator's tongue from straying.

The village park is used for the photographs, rhododendrons providing a deep purple backdrop. Anti Ceridwen tells Seth loudly that it's time he took some lucky girl down the aisle. Anti Delyth joins in, "Are you going steady yet?" The two sisters agree with one another that Seth would make some girl a good husband. They share their observations with anyone within earshot who can understand Welsh. Seth smiles at his aunts but beneath the smile are thoughts miles from their delusions. But he plays the family game, one last time.

The newly-weds drive off at about half past four, signalling the end of things. No evening bash. Naomi had been to too many weddings where everything seemed to drag into a drunken all-nighter. The reception had been fine, with good food and everyone on strict orders to keep speeches short. There'd been a lot of laughter. Robby had camped up a bit when he'd had the stage, but his contribution was polished and funny. He'd even learnt two sentences of Welsh, which were applauded wildly.

Back at the house Seth changes into jeans and a sweater and carries his few things out to the car. Mostyn joins him on the pavement in front of the house, "Thanks for making the family whole on this special day." He puts out his hand to be shaken.

Seth shakes his head; "The family wasn't whole Dad, not when I've had to pretend to be someone that I'm not! How can the family have been whole when the person I live with and love is excluded because of yours and Mam's misguided sense of what was right?" Seth flushes, gulps "Goodbye" and turns away.

Freddy Mercury's The Great Pretender is playing on auto-repeat along the Mawddach to Dolgellau and beyond. Passing through Bala without a stop, Piaf's *Non, je ne regrette rien* persuades Seth to leave whatever lingering doubts he harbours deep in the surrounding mountains. At Penyffordd, where the dual carriageway begins, Seth aches for Jude's touch of reassurance. He begins to welcome the freedom that Liverpool, just half an hour away, has helped him claim.

Jude isn't home. Alongside his note there's an envelope addressed to them both. The card inside announces: *Jude Canter and Seth Williams, Eli and Nina Canter request the pleasure of your company at the wedding of their daughter Louise, to Joshua Rosenberg.*

Eucharist

Kneeling at the communion rail, I wondered if it had been a free choice. In as much as any choice could be free, I supposed that it was so, but then people are always influenced by outside forces. Social norms, religious myths and beliefs, the political breezes of the age.... But yes, loving men in that way, and loving Joel in particular, finally hadn't felt right; out of tune, somehow, with the sacred music inside. The priest, Dafydd, was at the other end of the rail administering the Sacraments. I knew him professionally and we'd even met at a few social events, but our acquaintance wasn't a friendship that could share such secrets.

It had been twelve years since I'd last looked into Joel's open, wise face. We'd kissed and said goodbye again, for hadn't we been saying goodbye for weeks? In twelve hours the plane landed at Heathrow and I'd taken the train to my new home and a new job. We wrote, regularly to begin with, but the letters stuttered into infrequency as time passed. Joel's parish responsibilities had increased, while my own life also took on a crazed busyness as I embraced the challenge of ministering to six congregations.

Mrs Efans, a member at Bethania in the village, had been the post woman for forty years. "*Un o San Francisco heddiw Mr Llwyd,*" she'd say, handing me letters posted in the city that had been my home. Gwenda, as I was later invited to call her, had taken to knocking my door to hand-deliver in the first weeks after I'd arrived. In her eyes, such regular contact with the new minister back from America gave her status in our isolated, closed community. She had noticed that I wore my shirts open at the chest, showing all my hair, that my coffee mugs declared jokey slogans and that I listened to rock music.

I spilled my coffee on reading that Joel was dead. His most recent letter, in July last year, had told of a move to Boston. A letter full of excitement and hope in new beginnings… new movies to look out for and recent productions at the San Francisco Opera. Nothing to suggest a slowing down. Not a hint of ill health. No tell tale signs of being one of the thousands of worried well. The letter from Cheryl was unexpected and, once opened, unwelcome. She'd seen him in November, Kaposi's Sarcoma disfiguring his gentle face and the first signs of dementia cracking his intelligent, sometimes highbrow conversation. He'd died a few days before Easter. I wanted to cry. I wanted to hold Joel within that same strong tenderness we'd shared for nearly four years, to look into his face again and say, "I love you." A coffee stain edged further into the whiteness of the tablecloth.

I sought the sanctuary of routine, washing up the few dishes lying used by the sink. I placed the coffee stained tablecloth in a bucket of cold water. The gas bill was opened and processed for the next Presbytery meeting. I stripped my bed and loaded the washing machine. But as the possibility of routine's sanctuary gave way to despair, I sat in the window seat, with its view of Glan y Mawddach and Garn Gorllwyn across the wide estuary, and wept.

With no more tears but a heaviness that was hard to shoulder, I walked up into the hills behind the village and sat searching into the waters of Cregennen. I wondered when Joel might have picked it up. Surely since the days of our intimacy? In all the years of celibacy I'd never considered the possibility that the virus might be harboured somewhere in the nucleus of a white blood cell. But now the possibility gnawed.

Walking along Ffordd Ddu, I yielded to God's embrace and lying in the sun I breathed in the rich smells of heather, bracken and sheep droppings. The Healer, who'd always tended the wounds of my lifetime's struggle with a sexuality that was generally despised and mistrusted, comforted and re-assured my troubled mind. The sun warmed my face, inviting my imagination to wander again with Joel in the California sun. The camping trips to Yosemite... the retreats at the house in Bodega Bay where we'd read Anne Sexton and Dylan Thomas aloud to one another to ease the mental fatigue brought on by heavier theological tomes, and where we'd made love in the hot tub on the deck under the stars. I remembered the pumpkin festival at Half Moon Bay; the garlic ice cream in Gilroy that had made Joel sick... and the peace of the Rose Garden in the Berkeley Hills, shattered by the Argentinian students' demonstration against the Malvinas war. And I wept again, but now the tears were less bitter. I had come to appreciate that what I'd shared with Joel had been a rich gift.

That spring evening, in the vestry of Bethania, only six gathered for the mid week prayer-cum-bible meeting — *y seiat*. We read Psalm One Hundred and Sixteen together. Some of it had come to me, mouthed over and over, during my mind's sojourn with Joel, and again as I climbed down from the hills to the village late in the afternoon. Words that had been the source of comfort and strength to troubled people for more than two thousand years, had also comforted me. Gwenda Efans took her neatly ironed handkerchief from the shambles of her handbag. Wiping away the silent tears she told how she'd recited the same Psalm, from memory, to her comatose husband in Bangor hospital.

Gwenda's words recalled for me the cavernous pits of grief into which she and many others in my congregations had descended over the years at times of loss. The fatal car accidents; the terminal cancers; the two cot deaths in one family, suicides and so many divorces. I'd walked alongside, and sometimes quite literally held up so many who'd experienced lost hope, uncertain faith and the wrenching hurts of separation. I realised that the news of Joel's death had sparked none of these within me.

The *seiat* ended with cups of tea, relaxed conversation and Dilys Morris-Jones the newsagent's bara brith. After we'd talked, drunk tea, and eaten; all the rituals done, people made their way home. After locking up the building, I walked back to the manse intending an early night.

Cheryl's letter lay open on the table. The sight of it brought Joel back to me. Sitting, watching the lights across the estuary play on the waters of the in-coming tide, I began to make some sense of my feelings. I was sad about Joel's death, but not grieving for him, for hadn't I already grieved the loss of our relationship at the time of my return to Wales? But I was shocked that Joel had been infected with HIV and that he'd developed AIDS. And I was anxious — even afraid, because our communion had been carnal at a time before safer sex and condoms had become routine.

I got the number of the National AIDS Helpline, dialled without hesitation, and spoke with the counsellor. I had to stifle my need to persuade her that Joel couldn't have been HIV positive all those years ago. Her voice was pacifying, but my anxiety only deepened when she said that she couldn't speculate as to when he'd been infected. She talked to me for a long time about testing. The implications of a positive or negative result, how the choice had to be informed, and that before deciding to be tested I'd need to have some fairly clear idea of what I'd do if the result were positive. She was patient and understanding; I could hardly take it all in. She gave me the phone number of a clinic at the hospital in Wrexham where the test could be done. It was past midnight when I hung up the phone.

My blood was drawn off and the small glass vial was sealed in a plastic bag marked BIOHAZARD in bold, red letters.

"It will be a week before the result comes back, Iwan," the nurse said in broad Glaswegian. "You do have to come back to get the result. We don't give HIV results by letter or over the phone."

The doctor had been careful, before taking the blood, to establish that it was legitimate to test me and she'd asked about risky behaviours... unprotected sexual intercourse... shared injecting equipment.

"Risky gay sex then," she said as she wrote on the anonymous file.

The tears that blurred my vision and forced me into a lay-by on Llandegla Moors betrayed the first conscious realisation that I'd been hurt by the everyday language of the clinic: risky gay sex was an abridged version of all that I'd shared with Joel.

Routine carried me for seven days. The doctor was solemn when she confirmed the positive result of the blood test, and Ali, the Glaswegian nurse held my hand for some time; he was very tender. Somewhere, inside white blood cells, deep within the tissues of my body, there was a piece of biochemical grammar that had the potential to write a sentence in my genes, an instruction that would bring on cell death. The virus, coursing through my blood, waited for tomorrow. As it had done in Joel, tomorrow or some other tomorrow, it would cause my body's immune system to fail.

High above the village I made for the waters of Cregennen and the solitude that the mountains offered. I yearned for a quietness of mind, but a patchwork of thoughts had been woven in the hours since I'd been told, and my emotions lurched chaotically. Anxiety... confusion... joy... despair. The beauty and quiet of the mountain lake, shimmering in the early morning sunlight, were not infectious, and the thought looms continued to weave. I sought to grasp at the joy that my choice of celibacy now brought. The certainty that the virus, which lay dormant, had infected no one since my return from San Francisco.

"This is the Bread of Life," Dafydd said, standing before me and placing the wafer on my out-stretched palm. It stuck to my tongue. Somewhere, in a distant cavern of my mind, I heard the echoes of my own prayers over the elements, on the one Sunday in the month that my tradition allowed. "One Bread, One Body, One Lord of All, One Cup of blessing which we bless." Anxiety and confusion gripped me as the wine dislodged the wafer from my tongue....

"This is the Blood of Christ."

Joel came to me, offering comfort. I reached for the warmth of his touch. But the solace of his presence dissolved into the sorrowful words of Cheryl's letter, describing the cancer and dementia that had killed him. I swallowed, knowing that through my Communion, the Body of Christ would become infected. And with a pain that paralysed, the thought looms wove into the fabric of my being the first of many malignancies. Joel, too, had been blighted by my love.

Food For Thoughts

"A priest for God's sake!" Uwe's irritation was tinged by a heavier accent than usual. "Why didn't you mention it before so we could have discussed it?" Vivid images from his years at a Catholic boarding school near Aachen flashed before him. The priests had drunk themselves celibate, then taken delight in spanking the naked bottoms of pubescent boys with a slipper, while railing against masturbation and the sins of the flesh. What had Tecwyn been thinking about? A litany of expletives competed with the chopping of an onion on the hardwood board. He always swore in his mother tongue; it was more expressive, coming from his guts. And besides, when he swore in English the silly-sounding words made him laugh. With one swipe of the knife across the chopping board he heaped the onions into the pan with the oil, garlic and chillies and through the hissing, muttered "*Arschloch*."

Tecwyn smiled and handed his lover a gin and tonic, then, with a tap on Uwe's bottom and a blown kiss, said, "Some arse-holes are very nice!"

Uwe smiled sardonically: "So who is this priest you've invited for dinner?"

Tecwyn described Nick the Vic, so dubbed by his group of early-bird swimmers. The black hair and brown eyes; the power of his breaststroke across the near deserted pool; his banter in the changing room, always too cheerful for that time of the morning; the Prince Albert that he sometimes tugged just to tease the ones who stared lustfully at him in the shower.

"So why did you invite him?" Uwe asked. "Surely not because of his muscles, or is it some fascination for a forbidden piece of fruit with the ring through his *Schwanz*?"

Tecwyn steered the conversation into more serious waters, asking, "Isn't the whole point of tonight that we hear as many views as possible; to help us decide?" He thought for a moment and elaborated, "Since Nick is gay, he should understand our situation. Since he's a priest, maybe he can help us thrash out the heavy moral stuff?" With that he carried the tray of newly polished silverware into the dining room, leaving Uwe to start shelling the Dublin Bay prawns.

Uwe Greven, a consultant physician in genito-urinary medicine and pretty ace cook, had lived for six-going-on-seven years with Tecwyn ap Eifion who couldn't toss a salad unsupervised and was the only male family planning consultant working in Wales. They'd met at a Millennium Eve party, spent the first three days of the new century in bed together, and were an item by Valentine's Day. Both were out in every aspect of their lives. At work neither had felt it an issue, but then AIDS had brought lots of gay men into GUM. In Family Planning, being gay seemed to be a real advantage as it was non-threatening to the majority of women who'd traditionally cornered the field. At home, the house they'd bought and done up together bore all the hallmarks of fine taste, made affordable by considerable investment from their ample joint income. They loved their home, and loved to share its comforts with houseguests.

In their wider family life Uwe and Tecwyn realised their good fortune too. The Grevens, despite their Catholic piety, had demonstrated their acceptance of the situation with grace and showed genuine affection for Tecwyn through Christmas and birthday gifts. Tecwyn's mother, Arfona Lewis liked Uwe more than her two current sons-in-law, one of whom she found stupid, the other she considered pompous and English. She shared with him a love of opera, especially the Germans. In the four years since being widowed it was she, not Tecwyn, who accompanied Uwe to the Welsh National's two seasons at the Liverpool Empire and Opera North's at The Lowry. They'd even travelled to Bayreuth together for The Ring, leaving Tecwyn to tend his garden, feed her cats and work on the gay novel he was hoping to enter for one of the major prizes in the National Eisteddfod.

From the kitchen, Uwe asked, "Nia is coming tonight, isn't she? Doesn't she study ethics or moral philosophy?"

"I think so," Tecwyn replied, "but she's been invited because Judith's a lawyer... we need some lesbian input."

"So Mike and Tara are the token straights, then, are they?" Uwe surmised, totally unconvinced by the whole idea.

Coming back into the kitchen Tecwyn threw the tea towel he'd been using to wipe stray fingerprints from the silver at Uwe.

"Of course!" he exclaimed. "And before you ask any more stupid questions, Richard and Penri are coming because they're the gay men we've been friends with longest. And Arfona is my mother!"

Cutting the pork fillets lengthways to make pockets that would later be stuffed with prunes and sultanas, Uwe asked, "Has it ever struck you that our dinner guests might think we're being selfish? Perverse? What do we do if they're all against our idea?" It seemed to Uwe that to go ahead after soliciting their friends' opinions and meeting their disapproval would surely be worse than just doing it and letting them all find out later. Tecwyn answered, "Why should any of them disapprove? Besides, the whole point isn't to ask anybody for permission!"

Tecwyn dug up the parsnips, leeks and carrots that Uwe wanted to roast in goose fat. He cut some young sprigs of rosemary, lifted two heads of garlic and pulled a bunch of parsley from the herb garden. All the time he kept wondering if Uwe was right; that really it was no one's business but their own. Since they'd virtually decided to go for it, they might just as well get on with it. Uwe would hit forty before Christmas and he'd be thirty-six in the spring; they couldn't leave it too long.

Arfona Lewis had unpacked her overnight bag and was already helping Uwe in the kitchen when Tecwyn came in with the herbs and vegetables. She kissed her son and addressing him in Welsh asked, "How was your week? Have you any more of your manuscript for me to proofread?"

Tecwyn wondered what she'd make of the sexual encounter his main character had enjoyed with a man in a gay sauna. Tecwyn had become so sexually aroused writing it that he'd virtually dragged Uwe to the floor, where their own sex had been as greedy as anything he'd written into Iolo Pawl's adventures. Before Tecwyn could answer his mother, she'd taken the basket of vegetables, and was asking Uwe, "Have you got a knife? How d'you want them cut?"

Sitting across the kitchen table, Tecwyn watched his mother as she peeled and chopped. He wondered whether to forewarn her about the sex scene before handing her the pages, but he found it difficult to talk to her about sex. He appreciated the absurdity of his reticence; didn't he spend all his working hours talking quite comfortably about condoms, pills and other useful things with the safety-conscious sexually active? Perhaps he didn't need to say anything. Hadn't she surprised and shocked the critics with her last novel? The only one of the five she'd written which dealt with anything explicitly sexual, it was the story of a fifty-something widow's aching need for the intimacy her husband's death had stolen from her. Tecwyn remembered the unease with which he'd read of this older woman's search to quench her sexual thirst and wondered what elements of his mother's own story were woven into it. Unlike her heroine, who'd experienced a sexual reawakening, the flings of Arfona's own grief had left her depressed and unsatisfied. The intensity of her feelings had been deepened by her inability to talk to anyone about them. She still felt a searing lack of intimacy in her life.

"I'll put the new chapter on your bed-side table," Tecwyn

answered his mother, handing her a drink. "I'm going to take a shower."

She smiled as he set the glass on the table beside the mound of peelings, saying, "I'm looking forward to reading it!"

Uwe folded the dough over the sun dried tomatoes and worked the sticky mess for a few minutes, adding the odd fistful of flour until all the olive oil had been incorporated, and shaping it into two loaves. He knew already, from the feel of the dough, that the bread would be good. He set the loaves on the shelf above the Aga to prove.

"I'm having a shower now and then I'll take a nap until later on," he told Arfona. "There'll be time enough for everything else that we need to do."

Uwe pushed into the steaming shower alongside Tecwyn and pulled himself against the hardness of his back, his hands exploring — stroking and touching. In all their years together, neither had tired of the delight they took in each other's bodies. Each was free to "play"; they'd agreed in their first months that, given their respective histories with men, sexual fidelity would be irksome. It was a freedom they both valued, but never claimed, though neither knew it because each had agreed to spare the other the details. Tecwyn turned and they kissed deeply. And the sex they shared was good: it said "*Ich liebe dich... Rwy'n dy garu di...* I love you..." in ways that tired words in any language no longer could.

Through the half-sleep that came before the radio voices at five, Tecwyn's certainty about the dinner party gave way to the misgivings Uwe had planted. Why was he being so solicitous? He had seen the seemingly endless queues of young women and girls who came to his clinics. Though their thoughtlessness and irresponsibility often made him depressed and angry, he sometimes envied their possibilities. And perhaps, deep within him, what he craved was the permission to realise such possibilities for himself. But whose permission? And he wept when he realised it was the permission he failed to grant to himself. Feeling suddenly vulnerable he pulled himself against Uwe and held him.

Arfona sank into the over-stuffed armchair in the bay

window of the guest room; she liked its wallpaper and the view across the Dee and considered it her room whenever she stayed with the boys. She read the chapter her son had left on her bedside table. It irritated her that his Welsh was still not perfect. After all, he'd had the benefit of a Welsh language education — which was more than she could say for herself. She'd had to sit down and learn the grammar, making a conscious effort to use and write the language. She read with intense concentration, correcting the frequent errors but barely taking in the content of the piece. Only slowly did the awareness of Iolo Pawl's sexual experience dawn upon her. She wasn't shocked by what she'd read of these characters' antics. On realising, though, that the words and actions they described were conjured up by Tecwyn's imagination, she began to wonder if what he'd described were the kind of things he did with Uwe. It stung her that she'd begun to think about what her boys did sexually and she became uneasy. But curiosity displaced unease and she re-read the piece thinking all the time about Uwe and her son.

When she'd finished reading she looked out on the river, barely visible in the fading light, and sought to interpret her thoughts and feelings. She was mildly ashamed of what she felt was her voyeurism. Yet, putting this aside Arfona felt a certain liberation from a fear she had never fully realised. Reading her son's prose, she'd come to see that what two men might do together wasn't that much different from what she and her husband, Eifion had enjoyed. She smiled as she recalled the experimentation the sexual revolution of the 1960s had invited. They'd been sexually naive students at Bangor University then and the uninhibited exploration of one another's bodies had become their act of rebellion against the stifled sexual mores of their parents' generation. The thrill of Eifion's tongue on her clitoris for the first time... her first taste of his semen.... And she laughed quietly, remembering the student demonstration in London when they'd bought a dildo from a sex shop near Carnaby Street so that they could both feel what anal sex would be like before trying it out properly. The comfort of the armchair suddenly seemed to close over her... suffocating. Arfona Lewis yearned for her dead husband's lovemaking; she thanked whatever god that listened to silent prayers that Tecwyn and Uwe had each other.

Pouring more brandy over the pears and checking the loaves in the oven, Uwe wondered fleetingly if Arfona was becoming a bit unhinged. Coming down from her nap she'd given him the longest hug, a kiss, and said she loved him. It just wasn't her way. Her piano playing from the lounge hijacked his thoughts. Relishing the memory of a Chopin recital at the Bridgewater Hall he put the goose fat to warm and went down to the cellar to select the wines. Back in the kitchen he found Tecwyn sticking his fingers into pots and bowls, tasting, a crime punishable by finger amputation with the sharpest cleaver Uwe owned. Tecwyn left the kitchen in a hurry and went to check that there were enough fresh guest towels in the downstairs bathroom.

Richard and Penri were the first to arrive, immaculate, like models from some Paris autumn show. Close on their heels came Nick Bassham, all black leather and smiles, a tattoo of Celtic knot-work around his left wrist and not at all what Uwe had expected. As Tecwyn sorted their drinks, the phone rang; Tara and Mike would be late because the baby-sitter got the time wrong. Tecwyn winked at Uwe as he did his best imitation of a waiter and passed around the glasses: he'd won his bet again for those two were always late. Judith and Nia arrived; two beautiful women, elegant and understated, their skins tanned and hair sun-bleached after a holiday in Sri Lanka. And shortly after the appearance of the late arrivals, all moved into the dining room.

Much later, when they lay again in one another's arms, they un-picked the patchwork of the evening. Mike and Tara had talked about all the orphans the coalition against world terrorism had created. They saw a degree of madness in technological developments that made death for tens of thousands as unthinking a task as pressing the buttons on a dishwasher, and yet turned the creation of life itself into a well-refined laboratory technique.

Judith went on about how she'd acted for forty or fifty women, mostly lesbians, who'd made contracts with gay men in the few years since the successive New Labour administrations had changed the laws on surrogacy. The going rate was between thirty and fifty thousand Euros, plus expenses, and for some lesbian women it had been a way of tapping into the pink economy that had made so many gay men wealthy. Arfona had said something about love being all it takes to make a family, which was probably true but came out like trite drivel. Penri's preoccupation with designer things, from clothes to garden furniture, left no room in his and Richard's life for anything except the most chic; he kept interrupting the conversation with exaggerated compliments about their fine dining.

Uwe had liked Nick Bassham from Bodega Bay; he'd enjoyed his stories. He was Californian, and fulfilled all the stereotypes. What other society, Uwe wondered, could produce a sperm-donating gay Episcopalian priest whose beautiful body was adorned with tattoos and piercings? An initial point of contact, Uwe's love of Hitchcock's *The Birds*, filmed at Bodega Bay, had sustained his interest in Nick throughout the dinner. Nick had presented the ethical objections to the recently licensed reproductive technologies as though delivering a three-point sermon. The humanitarian, the aesthetic and the religious were examined, and though Nick said nothing he and Tecwyn hadn't heard before, Uwe had appreciated his clarity.

Finally, tiring of their whispered conversation under the duvet, Tecwyn nuzzled closer into Uwe's cradling body and caught the musk of his warmth. It excited him. In time, Uwe sensed the rousing in Tecwyn and beckoned him. Their bodies moved over one another and in their communion Tecwyn knew what possibilities were theirs to be realised. Catrin would be a lovely name for a daughter... but would they spell it with a C or a K?

Between the Devil and the Virgin

Gareth sat with his back against the ramparts, eight hundred feet above the valley floor. He peered intently through squinted eyes into blurring haze, trying to identify the familiar landmarks. The golf course, bounded by the Dee, was obvious enough and knowing the line of the canal, that too took its place in the shimmering vista. Further east, where the narrow boats chugged for a fifth of a mile across Telford's aqueduct, a hundred and twenty feet above the river, not one of the nineteen arches were visible in the smudged Turner landscape. Up the valley to the west, the Cistercians had built their abbey in the Valley of the Cross, but a blotch of woodland concealed the ruins. His *nain* always called the place Llyn Egwestl. He could just make out the cottage where she'd been born and lived all her life. Remembering the Sunday teas, he felt himself slide even further into the pathos of nostalgic memories. He got to his feet and willed himself out of the self-pity that had tinged the edges of his day since breakfast.

To impress her mother, Beth-Ann had squeezed fresh orange juice and warmed a bag of Sainsbury's croissants. There was unsalted French butter, a jar of good blackcurrant jam and a box of deluxe muesli. Gareth quipped something about Aldi not being good enough any more and she gave him a look that could kill, mouthing, "Shut up and eat." Louise pretended not to notice and became a loud American, effusive about her daughter's efforts and the sunshine streaming through the kitchen window. The coffee, dark and continental, had carried Gareth back to the café on the Piazza Anfiteatro in Lucca and a much happier time with Gwion. Louise distracted him, wanting to know what to look out for in Liverpool, but as their breakfast progressed Gwion broke through her prattling and Gareth felt the bleakness of their estrangement seep through him.

He declined Louise's invitation to go and be a tourist with them, thinking he'd be miserable company. As he washed up the breakfast dishes, though, he realised that being on his own all day would only make him feel more depressed and he began to regret his decision. Then the idea came to him that he could cycle himself out of it; strong physical exercise would get the hormones pumping around his body and lift his spirits. In less than an hour Gareth had crossed the bridge and was cycling along quiet country roads around the old estate to meet the lane that followed the river Clywedog up to Esclusham Mountain. There he'd take the forestry track to World's End.

It was a hot day. He stopped once by the river to quench his thirst and consider the remains of the Offa's Dyke, which stood tall across the hillside before him, the evenly spaced trees along its ridge like sentries. Smearing his neck and legs with sun cream, he recalled the day that he and Gwion had rambled that section of the Dyke footpath with Beth-Ann and some of their friends from college. The memory darkened his mood, but he mounted his bike again, trying to put Gwion out of his mind. The steep pull up the mountain and the rough track across the moor were strenuous and crueller than he'd remembered, but he felt wonderfully alive from the physical effort and recognised his growing well-being. Gareth's thoughts flowed freely, settling here and there like insects. He hummed melodies in time to the rhythm of his pedalling and marvelled at the stonechats that sang from gorse bush perches, launching themselves occasionally into sky dances, their white collars and red breasts lucid against the gilded upland. Still the track took him higher to where the grouse chattered their distinctive "go-back go-back" in the heather and a pair of peregrines soared, stooped and swooped. He stopped to watch their acrobatics and the muscles of his thighs and calves, jolted from their perpetual motion, twitched eagerly. On the crest of the open moor the sun was fierce. He thought of the forest; its shade seemed elusive, there on top of the world, but soon the fast and breezy descent brought him steeply down into the pine-scented coolness.

World's End gouged its course between Craig y Forwyn and Craig y Cythraul. Half way up the great limestone gorge, between the virgin and the devil, in amongst the relics of ancient mineshafts and limekilns, a spring bubbled up through the fallen boulders. Gareth knew it well from his childhood and splashing through the ford, where the stream from the spring crossed the track, he was thrilled to find it had not been parched by the hot, dry weather.

After hiding his bike in a clump of bracken he climbed up the gorge and found the pool, just below the spring, deep in the shadow of the soaring rocks. It was smaller than he remembered. He'd seen no one for more than an hour and feeling secure in his solitude he kicked off his trainers and peeled away the tee-shirt and shorts from his sweat soaked body. Reaching into the blue patch of sky above the gorge he stretched and tensed the muscle groups up and down his body, holding them taut and then slowly releasing the tightness. He repeated his cool-down a couple of times and was thrilled by the intense torrents of energy that surged through him. He brushed his nipples with the palms of his hands until each drupe hardened. Shocks sparked deeply, sending his body tingling. His right hand lingered at his chest, tracing the outlines of each firm pectoral, the fingers playing through the fine covering of hair. With his left hand he cupped his testicles, caressing them gently and intoxicating himself with the delight of it.... Then the coldness of the pool engulfed him. Gareth gasped for air.

Sobered by the cold penetrating his body, he lay on the grass for some time in a narrow shaft of sunlight. He bathed in its warmth until one persistent feeling invaded his calmness: the hunger for physical intimacy that had reawakened inside him. Gwion had been indifferent towards him for a while before their fight, not even wanting to cuddle. Gareth wondered if it really might be over; that in going away for the weekend to avoid him,

Gwion was really telling him as much. He wanted so badly to say sorry and try to salvage their life together. But if Gwion had already made his decision to move on, where did that leave him?

The narrow lane from World's End wound tortuously between high hedges of blackthorn, elder and wild honeysuckle, with overhanging foxgloves and stinging nettles that rasped and nipped at his legs. His progress was slow, for the blind corners made hard cycling foolhardy, but his mind raced: Gwion; sex… the possibility of being single again. Running up to Castell Dinas Brân had been a whim; he'd thought that the adrenalin rush might just pull him from the doldrums.

Moving away from the ramparts, Gareth caught a glimpse of the boy; he sat in the shade cast by one of the few arches that had endured the centuries of battle, siege and neglect. Each time Gareth glanced in his direction the boy's eyes were on him. Anticipation and possibility stirred and provoked the desires that had welled up inside him at the pool. He glanced again — and again, each contact with the boy's eyes willed the prospect of intimacy. On the crown of a small rise, Gareth turned to face the boy, held his gaze, and smiled. The boy smiled and nodded.

They headed off towards the thicket where Gareth had hidden his bike, between two piles of forgotten fencing stakes long ago wrenched from the ground, when small fields went out of agricultural fashion. There were no courteous pleasantries:

"What do you like?" Gareth asked.

"This and that," the boy said, with a trace of discomfort.

"I didn't bring any condoms," Gareth said, gesturing that the boy take in the Lycra shorts and tee-shirt and realise he was on a cycle ride.

"I've got some, but I'm not sure I want to do that," the boy said, unbuttoning his shirt and pulling it free from his shorts.

"Do you give, or take?"

"When it's okay… with the right person, I mean, then I like both."

"I don't take it. I like to be fingered really gently… but nothing inside! Do you like to be sucked?" Gareth noticed the line of hairs down from the boy's navel, cut sharply by the band of his shorts, and sensed his excitement at the prospect of what he'd find at their source.

"Yes," the boy smiled, "that's what I like best. And I like to suck too."

In the cool heart of the thicket they stood naked before one another. The boy's kissing was eager, but his hands clumsy, touching and stroking Gareth where his own had explored and delighted earlier, by the pool. Gareth felt the boy's hardness on his thigh, then between his legs, joshing; teasing and delighting. And then the boy's tongue sucked at his nipple.

"I'm Gareth," he whispered into the boy's ear.

"I'm Dan," the boy whispered back.

Gareth's gluttony for the boy's body wasn't near to being sated when the grunted orgasm spilled, surprising and disappointing him. He drew away without looking at Gareth, reached into the long grass for his shorts and pulled them on. Gareth, spitting out the bitterest semen he'd ever tasted, felt the frustration rise through him and he blurted out, almost angrily, "That's pretty selfish of you... just to leave me like this." The boy looked startled and turned away.

And then, reaching for his own shorts, everything in Gareth's mind fractured into a sequence of frozen frames. Dan was bent low. He raised a stubby fencing picket above his head, holding it with both hands. He seemed to be yelling at him but all Gareth heard was a whisper: "You fucking bastard of a cock-sucker." Then the jolting shock of realisation and a dull pain as the stake splintered and shattered over him. Then the surprise in Dan's mean, blue eyes... the fear in his face as he turned and ran.

Gareth spat out spongy slivers of wood, pulpy and rotten. Time ceased as he picked a beetle from his pubic hair, the fragmented episode becoming only gradually animated in his daze. When the sequence of events began to flow with some coherence, he remained entirely still and imagined the whole of his body, sensing for the damaged and broken parts. The only soreness was around his right shoulder and over onto his chest. Almost imperceptibly he began to move the muscles and then rotate the whole joint. Only when certain that neither the clavicle nor scapula were broken did he look, and saw the reddish weal where the blow had struck. A small spider rooted amongst the fine, debris-strewn hairs on his chest.

Gareth heard the whispers and giggles from Beth-Ann's room and he wondered about disturbing them because he needed to talk. Cycling back from Llangollen, the encounter with Dan had been re-wound and played over and over. His first thought, still in the depth of the thicket as he'd dressed, avoiding the soreness in his shoulder, was that he'd provoked Dan. He'd tried to remember exactly what he'd said to the boy as he'd pulled away... how threatening had he seemed? Later, as he cycled, more sinister interpretations took shape in his mind. He needed to get another viewpoint, to put a check on his paranoia. He hesitated before knocking on Beth-Ann's door. Did he really want her to know he'd been so casual? Perplexed in his hesitation, he decided to shower. Under the jets of water that soothed his bruised shoulder, Gareth thought of Rhodri, an old lover. His training as a police officer would surely help to untangle the embellishments of his imagination and see the event for real. He felt sure, too, that Rhodri would be able to offer him consolation in ways that Beth-Ann might not consider.

They sat at a small table in a bay window with a view of the river. Rhodri, dark and thick set, drank his coffee, his left hand cradling his weekend stubbled chin. He flicked his left earlobe unconsciously, his index finger nicely manicured but crooked. Gareth smiled, remembering the endearing habit, and slurped the last of the Ferry Inn's house red from the over-large wine glass.

"I'd really like it if you'd come home with me," Rhodri ventured.

"That would be nice," Gareth said, still attracted to him and moved by the concern he'd shown. The stirring in his groin made him remember how good they'd once been together.

"Do have a think about what I said then," Rhodri urged, pressing his knee momentarily against the inside of Gareth's thigh in a gesture of reassurance before nudging it upwards provokingly. "If you want me to talk to one of the liaison officers in the

Community Protection Unit, just let me know. This kind of thing needs investigating, really. The next time this guy decides to hit someone over the head he might just do some real harm. Think hard on that, Gareth, please. Just imagine how you'd feel if his next victim...."

"I know that I should report it, Rhod," Gareth interrupted.

Rhodri's knee pressed gently again, the gesture calming.

"I can't really risk drawing that sort of attention to myself though, not in the kind of work I do," Gareth said, playing his fingers over Rhodri's knee. "It's all right for New Labour to have gays and lesbians in their London cabinet, but look what happened in the Assembly? And around here, you know as well as I do, that sort of thing just won't wash."

"Probably all the other men this weirdo has attacked feel the same way, so we don't ever get enough information to build up a case against him."

"Yea... yea... yea... so what is it about North Wales Police that's keeping your closet door so tightly shut?" Gareth jibed. "Put the shoe on the other foot, Rhodri and tell me what you'd do."

His silence confirmed Gareth's suspicion that the police did not easily perceive the gap between their own professional advice and personal practice.

For fifteen, maybe twenty minutes they lay together, exhausted in a sexually sated slumber. Gareth felt a residual dribble from Rhodri's shrunken cock; it trickled down his thigh, tickling, but he couldn't reach down to wipe it away because Rhodri lay across him. To distract himself he thought about the events that had led him to fall so willingly into Rhodri's arms: the stupid row with Gwion... the pent-up sexual frustration and his fling in the bushes with Dan that had left him bruised and shaken. Rhodri farted and Gareth sensed the shallowness of their intimacy. Feeling awfully alone, he wanted to be held by Gwion — and no one else.

Mischief and Deep Secrets

Morfudd Jones rocked the soggy stub of her third cigarette into a clean, pale blue patch of the Wedgwood ashtray — the one that Alwena Jones had given her for her birthday the previous September. It had come from a small but treasured collection of Jasperware, which Alwena displayed on the Victorian chiffonier in her room. Before, Morfudd had always used a heavy glass one that the home had grudgingly provided... though Matron generally disapproved and had made her promise that she wouldn't smoke in bed. After a sigh — that might have summed up how tiresome she found this awakening before five, or was perhaps just an expression of the disdain she felt at another day being added to the thirty odd thousand days she'd already endured — she wiped the drool that had dribbled down her chin onto her wizened breast with a crumpled tissue and heaved her stiff legs from beneath the covers. The first few steps were always a bit of a wobble now, but with a hand on the bedside table and the smooth curving mahogany of the vitrine that held her last few precious knick-knacks, she eventually steadied herself. With a straight back, she walked into the bay and pulled back the curtains.

It had rained again in the night: July was proving to be a washout. The Pines Rest Home stood on an exposed outcrop above the town, taking all the weather blown in off Cardigan Bay.

Morfudd sulked at the wild, white stallions that charged onto the sandy beach beyond the council houses and the heavy, grey clouds that closed the town in on itself. Perching herself on the arm of the easy chair where she sometimes sat to watch the life of the town through a pair of cracked binoculars, she started to day-dream. It was only when her red-ringed, rheumy eyes fell on the crescent rose bed in the front garden below her window that she remembered Buddug Jones.

Morfudd stood and looked around the large, airy room for the plastic carrier bag that she'd put down the evening before. She'd been affected when Buddug had become so upset by the wet weather ruining the roses and had persuaded Matron to let her go down into town in the van with Griff, but only on condition that she came back up in a taxi. Matron was like that; always extracting promises and setting conditions. She'd tried Woolworth and the flower shop by the station, and even ventured into the Bargain Centre in the old *Capal Wesla* — and to think they were selling pan scourers and German condoms on the very spot where the *Parchedig* Tomos Talfan Elias had christened both her boys. Feeling downhearted, Morfudd had nipped into the wine store and bought a bottle of Grouse so that her jaunt wouldn't be completely in vain. But then, on a stall in the market, run by an Indian woman with a spot of paint on her forehead and wearing jeans under her sari, she'd found what she'd been looking for. After her adventure in town, she'd feigned an overwhelming fatigue for the remainder of the day and closed herself in her room, leaving Alwena and Buddug to their soaps and their knitting. She'd ruined her nail scissors during the afternoon trimming a good foot off each of the stiff, plastic stems and cutting three-inch lengths from the roll of green garden wire. She spied the carrier bag nuzzled against the vitrine and with a sharp intake of breath she set about her little spot of gardening.

After placing the stupidly grimacing gnome from beside the pot of geraniums against the open front door so as not to lock herself out, Morfudd Jones set off across the lawn. The grass was soggy and it squelched between her gnarled toes. For a fleeting moment she wondered what the casual observer of her early morning expedition might conclude. Hesitating, she considered the wisdom of retracing her steps and changing from her nightdress, but then concluded that she should press on to the rose bed and get on with the job. On the stems that George, the handy man, had already dead-headed, Morfudd attached the short-stalked buds and blooms, pricking her fingers, hands and forearms as she bound the green garden wire tightly around the overlapping ends. Fixing the roses took much longer than she'd anticipated but no one interrupted her and she was back in her room by five to six.

Over the past months, Alwena Jones and Buddug Jones had both stopped putting on make-up, which saved them ten minutes in the mornings. They were already looking into their tea when Morfudd came into the dining room. It was Alwena's idea, to stop smoothing away the wrinkles with foundation and powder: "*Duw,* it's time we stopped plastering Polyfilla into the cracks... time to grow old disgracefully," she'd coaxed. Buddug, being the most weak-willed of the three, had followed suit after a short time. Morfudd, commenting frequently that they both looked like death warmed up, remained faithful to her Seamless Liquid Foundation in porcelain and her Sun Frolic crème puff, but her enthusiastic attempts to disguise the ravages of age often led to grotesque consequences. As Morfudd poured herself a cup of tea, Alwena noticed all the scratches from the rose bushes.

"You had your hands in Joseff-*Fferm*'s ferret bag?" she goaded.

Morfudd smiled, answering, "I've been sewing the buttons back onto my winter coat after it came back from the dry cleaners."

Buddug, who was more than a little deaf, said that her Michael was coming for tea.

"I hope he'll bring me some roses — that rain has spoiled all the ones in the crescent bed. Maybe he'll bring some Welsh cakes from Corner Café too!"

Alwena raised her eyes to the gods and wondered if senility was infectious. Morfudd peered between the two women, whose backs were to the window, and beamed at the crescent rose bed where the Deep Secrets and the Mischief swayed in the breeze off the sea.

"Your Michael is such a good boy, coming to see you like he does," she remarked, remembering the hundreds of Marlboro's he'd given her when he and his *friend* had resolved to give up smoking. The smile got lost in the slobbery burlesque line of Max Factor's Firebrand and her eyes dimmed beneath the smudged aquamarine eye shadow. She couldn't remember when her surviving son had last called to see her.

A while later, as Buddug and Alwena disagreed over an instruction in the knitting pattern, Morfudd wondered what had kept her Aled away for so long. She knew that being a solicitor was an important, busy job — and he and Melissa had, after all, seen to it that she was in a *private* rest home... though why she couldn't have gone into their granny flat was beyond her. Wasn't that what granny flats were for? But then, Melissa had her aerobics and her golf — and all her commitments on *the bench*. Feeling herself becoming despondent, she straightened her back and thought about how effeminately ridiculous Buddug's Michael was. It was a disgrace, how lovey-dovey he and his friend were. And thinking it was better to have no visitors at all than to be visited by ones quite so queer, she felt her spirits rise again.

When Michael and Gerard arrived just before three-thirty, with roses for Buddug, Welsh cakes for tea and a box of Thornton's for sharing around, Morfudd lifted her copy of *People's Friend* to within inches of her nose and made believe she hadn't noticed them... but she peeked now and then, and strained to hear their conversation. Michael, whom she dismissed as a balding, bulging, blubbering milksop, fussed for the first ten minutes over his mother's hearing aid — well, over the fact that she wasn't wearing it again — whilst Gerard, who looked so much like Gregory Peck, talked with Alwena about the latest twists and turns in *Coronation Street*. Morfudd could make herself feel quite sick if she thought too much about how indiscreet these boys could be, but sometimes she allowed her curiosity to get the better of her and she'd wonder which of the two wore the frocks and pinafores about the bungalow they lived in together. Gerard looked so manly that she couldn't conceive of him being the wife!

"I thought you said the roses in the front had been ruined with all the rain, Mam," Morfudd overheard Michael saying with a barb of accusation as he fussed, arranging the bunch of roses he'd brought his mother in a tall jam pot that one of the girls handed him as an excuse for a vase: "You've no need to be telling me porkies to get me to bring you flowers, you know." With this, Morfudd closed her magazine, wiped the ooze from her chin, and waited for events to unfold.

"But they are all spoiled," Buddug insisted, getting up with some difficulty and hobbling over to the window. "Poor George, who's taken such a lot of care with them, was out there yesterday — but...."

"See," Michael said with a full-of-himself 'I told you so'.

"*Brenin y bratiau*," Buddug exclaimed, the astonishment causing her to stagger and reach for the arm of Miss Perkins' chair to steady herself, "but only yesterday... I watched poor George dead-heading them."

"That wasn't yesterday Buddug *fach*," Morfudd put in mischievously, knowing that she could sometimes get a bit mixed up. "We both sat here watching George one afternoon last week... not yesterday. Come and sit down and open these chocs."

"How are you then Morfudd love?" Michael asked, guiding his mother back to her chair, his voice at too high a pitch, its modulation too singsong. Morfudd hated it that he called her love all the time, and that he was so brazen to think he could be on first name terms with her. "Not getting you all excited is it, love... that *People's Friend*? They tell me it's got quite a reputation for saucy stories."

"But it's been raining for days," Buddug said, her surprise giving way to an upset bewilderment, "and roses never do well in the rain."

"Come on Mam," Michael encouraged. "Sit down here and we'll all have a nice cup of tea."

"Oh — but they are lovely," Buddug said, turning to appreciate the roses in the crescent bed before Michael coaxed her back to her chair, where she sat, her head skewed awkwardly, trying to keep sight of them through the blur of cataracts. Morfudd sipped her tea and enjoyed the buttery taste of the cakes — and she feasted for a while on Buddug's childlike pleasure.

Before the gong went for dinner, Alwena Jones noticed the commotion outside. By the crescent rose bed, Kylie, one of the girls who came in to wash the dishes during the school holidays was screeching with laughter, while George leaned on his garden fork and scratched his head. Matron, bent low over a rose bush, was picking at a rosebud as if it was a dog's stinking turd, by the look on her face. Alwena roused Buddug and Morfudd from their magazines.

"I want them all taken off, George," came Matron's hysterical entreaty through the open window.

"What's she saying to George then?" Buddug quizzed.

"Oh, they look so cheap and nasty," Matron harangued. "Our residents here at the Pines don't pay for any kind of imitation, George... this isn't what you'd expect at a *private rest home* — you've been here long enough to know that." She held open a black plastic bin liner and gestured to him: "I want every one of them off, now!"

Buddug began to wail when she saw George and Matron vandalise the crescent rose bed. Alwena, though confused by what she was witnessing, leaned over and took Buddug's hand to comfort her. Morfudd, feeling Buddug's distress, got up from her chair and after steadying herself, walked to the window and rapped her knuckles hard against the pane until she captured the vandals' attention.

"Please stop that, Matron," she called through the open window with a determination that surprised Morfudd herself. "Those roses are giving Buddug, Alwena and me such pleasure.

Stop it immediately."

"But they're *plastic roses* Mrs Jones," Matron sallied forth, "artificial... not real."

"But from here they look beautiful Matron... and when you're over eighty, and your world has shrunk to the four walls of an *old people's home*, a little bit of beauty isn't a lot to ask for — even when it is an imitation."

"Mrs Jones *fach*, we're a *private rest home* —."

"And private means that *we* are paying, doesn't it Matron?" Morfudd interrupted with all the sharpness that her drooling tongue could cut, "so Buddug, Alwena and I would like you to leave the plastic roses just the way they are."

And the plastic roses in the crescent bed swayed on in the evening breeze.

Morfudd Jones and Alwena Jones watched the orange streaks fade in the sky over Bardsey Island and waited for the last of the less mobile residents to be escorted to their bedrooms. When they were finally alone, Morfudd poured a good joch of whisky into each of their cocoa stained mugs from the flask she kept in her handbag.

"You do some lovely things to keep Buddug's spirits up," Alwena offered by way of thanks as Morfudd passed her the mug.

"She's had so much disappointment in her life," Morfudd said, "especially the way that Michael of hers has turned out."

"But he comes to see her, Morfudd *fach*, which is more than I can say for any of my three," Alwena answered.

"My Aled comes when he can," Morfudd countered with an eagerness that betrayed her disillusionment. She wiped the spit from her chin and took a slug of whisky.

"Do you think about your Lewis sometimes?" Alwena asked after a while. "Now he was a lovely boy. He and our Nesta were very thick for a time... remember?"

"I never think about him!" Morfudd spat, and hoped that her tears would drown in her watery eyes.

"*Duw* — it's such a different world now," Alwena mused.

"You see them in the magazines all the time; boys with boys and girls with girls...."

Morfudd took another slug of whisky. Its fiery sharpness couldn't raze the memory of finding her Lewis hanging from a beam in the attic just hours after his father had bawled that no son of his —.

"Gerard was even telling me this afternoon that they've been accepted by the adoption panel," Alwena interrupted Morfudd's thoughtfulness. "They're hoping to make Buddug a *nain* before Christmas; now won't that be nice for her?"

Morfudd swallowed her revulsion and tried hard to force a smile.

Gifts

I watched Rhun as he skimmed through the glut of Christmas post. Among the round robins, those often meagre attempts to sum up "the year in the life of" were those from people we didn't particularly care about and hadn't seen for years. These he tossed aside after only a perfunctory glance. Some of the Christmas cards, however, brought smiles and joyful sighs. About half way through the stack he took a slurp of wine and quipped, "No surprises this year then?" He might have been anticipating a greeting from someone we'd lost touch with whose company we'd enjoyed or someone we'd fallen out with over something totally inane, but I knew he was thinking of an evening just like this exactly a year ago.

Krista's letter had arrived in an elastic-banded bundle. It was on the day I'd been looking out for Dewi-post to give him his Christmas box. Because my parents were coming to us for the holiday I'd taken a couple of days off work to clean the house (my mother is such a fastidious woman). I'd watched Dewi trudge up the lane through the sludge of the previous day's snow. He looked perished so I asked him in for a coffee or something — like you do at Christmas. He only stayed long enough to gulp down his tea: although he was curious enough about us, he was clearly uncomfortable to be alone in the house with me.

I must have read Krista's letter half a dozen times. The fact

70

that she'd deteriorated so quickly left me wondering if she'd skipped a year and the news of her daughter's coming out was already two years old. I hadn't known that diabetes could knacker your kidneys. The dialysis sounded awful and the wait for a kidney even more wearing. They'd been down the route of looking to her immediate family to see if one of them could donate. Phil, her husband, had high blood pressure and Hannah, like her mother, was diabetic. There was a brother who'd joined the Jehovah's Witnesses, so he hadn't even been asked to consider a blood test. So she was on a waiting list. She sometimes found herself daydreaming, especially around Bank Holidays and Christmas, that some wonderfully fit and healthy person would be fatally injured on the road so that she might regain her life. Waking from such daydreams, she'd come out in a cold sweat realising what a nightmare she was wishing on some anonymous family.

Throughout that day as I hoovered and dusted, made up the spare bed (I even ironed the sheets and pillowcases), bleached the loo and zapped the black scummy mould in the shower with stuff from one of those spray guns, I thought about Krista. We'd had a lot of fun together, and a lot of heartache too... half a lifetime ago.

Aberystwyth in the late seventies. We met at Welsh classes. I'd got it into my head that since I'd come to Wales to study I ought to learn my granny's mother tongue. I had little understanding of what I was taking on. Krista's motive seemed more lofty; she was into Celtic languages. She was into Abba and disco too... a real dancing queen. In those days it wasn't so easy to come out but by the middle of the first term Krista had sussed me. Walking down Penglais Hill one Saturday night after the disco in the union bar she asked me straight out. The alcohol had loosened both our tongues and by the time we reached the prom I was in floods of tears. Southport wasn't exactly the best place for a gay boy to grow up and come to understand himself. I was still very confused and still very much a virgin. We sat in a shelter by the bandstand for ages, just talking.

There was a sense of covertness about the Aber Gay Soc. There was no phone number, just a PO box in the old union building. Krista helped me write the letter. I didn't want it to sound too pathetic. It took more than a week for anyone to respond. I was invited to meet two of the members in the front bar of the Belle Vue... I could bring a friend if I wanted to. Krista held my hand.

I fell head over heels with Patrick and we had an intense couple of months. Krista consoled me when he went off with Jimmy. On the re-bound I found myself in bed with Hugh, one of the lecturers from organic chemistry, who must have been at least forty (though he kept himself in good shape). It was in the days after that frantic night of lusty tumble that I learned the meaning of the term chicken queen: Hugh liked them young and wasn't looking for love and I was just another weekend treat from the meat counter. Then Owain screwed me over and screwed me up and I started to hate gay life in Aberystwyth and wonder if it would always be that way.

That summer after our first year Krista and I went inter-railing. Every other night we slept on a train to save money. We managed a month in Europe, nine countries, fifteen big cities and one decent meal a day on a hundred and twenty-five quid each, money we'd saved from our grants. On the nights we stayed in hostels and cheap hotels, we shared a room and shared a bed, and whether it was something about being in foreign lands, or something in the air, we slept together. Well, more than just slept, I mean.

We carried on after the summer break, but back in Aber it didn't seem so romantic or so real somehow. Shagging on a single bed in the halls of residence, where you could hear everything through the walls, seemed to bring a different world upon us and being in familiar surroundings made me think again about being gay. A couple of weeks into the term I was seeing Tudor and feeling bad about two-timing Krista. Then, on a Wednesday in early November she said she'd missed her period. What did I know about contraception? I'd just assumed she'd sorted it. I behaved like a real shit. I even asked her if she was sure it was mine. We didn't see one another for ages after the abortion.

On a Saturday in January we bumped into one another in Galloway's and I persuaded her to come to the Cabin for a coffee. We talked and then walked the prom to kick the bar. She'd started seeing someone. I said I was glad. I also said I was sorry for all the hurt I'd caused her. She said she'd missed being friends with me. I said we could still be friends if she wanted, but it didn't happen. When we met, in the union refec or the back bar of the Skinners, we'd agree that we should do something together, but we never did.

A good few years after we'd graduated and moved on from Aber I saw her in a restaurant in Manchester. I was with Roger, an architect, the only married man I ever went out with. She was with a handsome, blond man and they looked all intimate, so I decided it would be better not to renew our acquaintance, but she caught my eye as we got up to leave. So I met Phil. They were celebrating their fourth wedding anniversary. We swapped addresses, but I didn't expect to hear from her. The next Christmas I got the first of her newsy round robins.

After cleaning all day and making a beef casserole ready for when Rhun got home, I lounged in the bath and wondered whether it was even possible for a live stranger to donate a kidney. Setting the table for dinner I stuffed Krista's letter into the middle of the heap so as not to draw attention to it and rehearsed the lines I might say to Rhun. He laughed, which really put me off my stride, and said that the chances of a cross match were so remote that I should save myself the bother. I said that if the chances were really so remote he wouldn't mind if I got a leaflet from the transplant centre in Liverpool.

Beryl George, the transplant coordinator, spoke to me via the switchboard.

"Live non-related donors aren't that common in Britain, but it happens a lot in America. I'll put some information in the post for you." She continued, "The first step would be to have a blood test to see if you've the same blood group as Krista. Make an appointment later on if you want to move things on."

I found the card from the Blood Transfusion Service in an old wallet full of bits and pieces. Before the whole AIDS thing, I'd given blood regularly but then they started advising those of us in high-risk groups against doing so. O positive. Then I went to the top floor of the Royal Liverpool Hospital to meet Beryl. Rhun pooh-poohed it all as a waste of her time and mine, but she took me very seriously. There was me thinking I was going for a bit of a chat and she says she might as well check me out. Weight... height... blood pressure... medical history... and some blood tests, just to check for a hundred and one things as well as any infectious diseases.

"Do you mean AIDS and stuff?" I asked.

"There's no point raising your friend's hopes if you're unsuitable from the word go because of things like CMV, Hepatitis B, Hepatitis C or HIV."

She gave me a couple of two litre containers and an instruction sheet to take away with me.

Rhun was hostile: "Are you going through a mid-life crisis? Why else would you want to do something so fucking crazy for someone who's practically a stranger?"

I answered him cautiously, "Once upon a time, in another life, I loved Krista. Perhaps, if you've loved someone once, they stay a bit special, you know?" It sounded trite and untrue, especially when I thought of all the men in my life. But that was the first time Rhun knew that Krista was more than just someone I'd known in Aber.

Beryl phoned to say that all the blood tests had come back and they were fine. I'd passed the first hurdle and it was now an appropriate time to put my offer to Krista. I looked them up in our Christmas card address book and wrote her a letter. She phoned me less than an hour after she'd torn the envelope open. She was O positive too... and did I really know what I was letting myself in for?

We started e-mailing. She wanted me to be open and honest with her, every step of the way. If I was going to embark on this journey she wanted all the gory details so that she could share it with me... and she wanted to know what I was thinking. And if I changed my mind it would be alright... she'd understand. Some of our e-mails were plain stupid. *You and Phil sure you're okay about a gay kidney,* I fired off one day. *Of course,* came the reply, *as long as it's healthy and working well... it'll give a whole new meaning to being gay friendly!*

Beryl made an appointment for me with the consultant physician and nephrologist and made the arrangements for more bloods that could be sent for cross matching with Krista's. I had to say something at work because I needed time off to drive to Liverpool. My boss said it was a noble thing I was doing, embarrassing me. The news came through that the match, though not perfect, was good enough, especially given that kidneys from live donors were preferable to ones from cadavers. If I wanted to go on I'd have to have an IVP and a renal artereogram, invasive procedures that required someone to accompany me to the hospital. Beryl suggested that perhaps Rhun would come with me: she wanted a chat with him.

As the weeks passed, Rhun had begun to realise that the chances were looking better and he'd stopped joking about it... in fact, he'd stopped talking about it altogether. When I asked him if he'd come with me to the hospital, the real possibility of it all hit him. He went ballistic.

"Why are you being so selfish?" he exploded. "Don't I matter any more? Don't you care what I think about it all... what I'm feeling? What if something goes wrong? Why d'you have to do this?"

I tried to articulate it. With Beryl it hadn't seemed so difficult but with Rhun I couldn't find words. "So you think you owe it to her, like repaying a bad debt?" he asked. I tried to explain what our relationship had been like... and the abortion. Being a gay man in my forties... no kids... leaving no real impression on the world… leaving nothing behind. What was happening with Krista was important and I had the opportunity to make a real difference in somebody's life.

Very quietly, Rhun said, "And you don't think you've made a real difference in my life?"

There were a few horrible days. I'd failed to explain my motives and Rhun curled up in his spiky shell and closed me out.

The appointment card came through for the IVP. It was a glorious Saturday morning in May and we'd planned a hike up the Rhinogs.

"What if you can't go on rambles afterwards?" Rhun quizzed with less hostility and more concern.

"Maybe, if you came with me," I said, gesturing towards the appointment card, "Beryl or Dr Williams would be able to answer your questions." He blew me a kiss across the table, responding more soberly, "I don't want you to do this, but I have to respect your right to follow it through. I'll arrange to take the day off."

The IVP was fine: a shot of dye in the arm and a series of X-rays that showed the venous structure of the kidneys. Beryl had her chat with Rhun, and in the next days he opened up much more. He downloaded articles that we discussed at length, especially the testimonies of those who'd donated kidneys. He seemed satisfied that the recovery rate for the donor was very good and that the one remaining kidney had the capacity to grow and compensate for the other.

"Beryl said that unless I was a hundred percent behind you she'd pull the plug on the whole thing," Rhun ventured one afternoon as we dug up potatoes. I asked him what had made him change his mind.

"A person willing to give a kidney to a friend is a pretty special kind of person and it's made me love you even more. Though I still think you're off your head!"

The renal artereogram was the last hurdle. A fine catheter was inserted under local anaesthetic into an artery in my groin, and then coaxed up towards the kidneys. Once in position, a dye was released to show the arterial structure of the kidneys. Some people have two arterial branches serving one or even both kidneys and that makes them unsuitable for removal; mine had one artery each. Lying flat on my back as still as possible for four hours afterwards was a bore. Rhun read the newspaper, flirted with the nurse who checked my blood pressure every twenty minutes and then went off to have lunch with Beryl.

The thumbs up came through in August and the surgery was set for the first Thursday in September. Work had given me a three-month paid special leave and as the news got around people stopped me in the corridors and in the canteen to say how brave... selfless... virtuous... and just plain fucking stupidly wonderful I was.

"You'd do the same for someone you loved," I'd fire back at them. "You would, wouldn't you?" And sometimes you could see it in their faces that they bloody well wouldn't.

The surgeon came around a couple of hours after I'd been admitted. He was younger than I'd expected. He talked with Rhun and me for a while, referring back to the notes he'd been sent from the Royal Liverpool. Then he did a physical examination and took my blood pressure.

"You're a bit anxious I expect," he said as he noted the numbers on my chart. He scanned the notes from Liverpool again. "There's no history of high blood pressure in your family is there?" With some puzzlement I said that there wasn't, as far as I knew, and wondered whether it was the fact that he was so fancyable that had excited me. He did the test again a few minutes on, and looked perplexed as he wrote the numbers down. Then he got someone else to do it and it was higher again. It levelled out by the middle of the afternoon at 180 over 120... and that's where it hovered for the three days that I stayed in the hospital.

I was depressed for about a month after my attempt to donate was aborted. Of course, Krista and Phil were gutted to have come so close, only to have all their hopes thwarted, but they were so nice with me. Rhun was wonderfully tender and kept assuring me that despite the thoughts in my head and the desires of my heart, my body finally said a very definite no… and that that was alright. I became preoccupied with notions of failure and for the first time in my life I questioned whether it was indeed better to have tried and failed than not to have tried at all. By the middle of October my blood pressure settled back down at 130 over 80 and I went back to work. People were kind and I tried to get back to normal.

Rhun must have said something to Krista and Phil about those bleak days. She sent me a letter, which arrived one austere November day.

You must think about what you have given to me and Phil, and not think about what couldn't in the end be given. I've grown used to being let down by my body over the years. Count yourself lucky that the way in which your body let us all down hasn't caused you any long-term physical harm. I know that you're upset, but please know and understand that the gifts you gave me this past year are priceless. You renewed my faith in the depth and breadth of friendship, you restored my trust in loyalty, you showed us kindness the like of which is never forgotten… and most of all you gave me something to hope for.

Rhun took another slurp of wine and reached for my parents' Christmas card, which I'd shoved towards the bottom of the bundle. Their Christmas gift to us, a cheque for five thousand pounds, fluttered to the floor as he opened it.

"I thought you said there were no surprises this year," he said with a hint of accusation.

The View from Sasso Fermo

The impressive fountain churned up in the wake of the twin-hulled *Carducci* quickly washed away the view of the landing stage, the palm trees and the boxes of mauve geraniums that adorned the wall along the lakefront promenade. Out of breath, Glain gripped the handrail to steady herself against the ferryboat's roll but as the surge of acceleration unbalanced her she slipped her arm through Cai's. Her silver streaked hair blew in all directions and the three points of the Hermes silk scarf tied around her neck flapped with manic indignity.

"We made it," she said after catching her breath, her voice rasping from too many cigarettes. "I really thought that we'd miss it and have to wait for the six-o-clock."

Cai smiled. It was the first time in many months that Glain had seen him smile and it made her more optimistic.

Once the boat had reached its cruising speed it was stable in the water and the passengers could walk about the deck with less caution. Glain began to relax and she spoke with a man in a white linen jacket who'd begun to show an interest in her. Cai moved to the side rail, leaned against its metallic smooth coolness, and gazed at the forested mountains that rose steeply from the water's edge. Seeing the ridges and gorges emerge from the afternoon shadows as the boat made its swift progress along the lake, he was eager to hike the trails he'd studied on maps the reception manager at the Villa Cannero had agreed to send when Glain had made their booking. In profile Cai was handsome: clear skin, a small, slightly pointed nose, the eye more grey than blue, which from a certain angle was shot through with turquoise, and jet-black hair worn almost cropped. He drew the wondering glances of men and women in equal measure.

Half smiling at the man along the rail to his right who'd begun to cruise him, Cai unconsciously drew his hand across the stubble of his left cheek before resting his chin in its wide palm. Even when closely shaven, his beard was dark and this pronounced the clean, white line, more surgical than accidental, that ran through his top lip, just up from the left corner of his mouth, and forged across his cheek to within a centimetre of his eye. It was impossible not to notice. It was what most people — strangers, even those initially attracted to his right profile — saw before turning away. The few not put off by such disfigurements, Some like Tudor, could see that the scar added interest, and even mystery to a face that the bitchier queens on the scene would have said was pretty.

Most of those who didn't turn away were still too embarrassed to acknowledge it... but Tudor had asked about the scar straight away. His forthright manner had taken me aback, but he had a way of putting you at ease. The first time we slept together he drew his fingers gently over it, 'kissed it better' and ran his tongue along its length. Even then, all those years ago, Tudor seemed to know about human fragility and understood that broken people needed a little extra gentleness. After we'd moved in together 'kissing it better' became a bit of a goodnight ritual.

"This is Max," Glain said, interrupting Cai's imaginary ramble in the mountains. "He's staying at Villa Cannero too."

"Hello," Max said with enthusiasm.

"Hi," Cai said, turning towards them. He offered the man in

the white linen jacket the broadest smile and began to think that perhaps Max might be his saviour. What had ever possessed him to come away with Glain?

Max flinched. He was unable to disguise the wince that momentarily twisted his photogenic features. He averted his gaze, focussed on the small Celtic cross that Cai wore on a chain around his neck, and said the first thing that came into his head: "Glain was just telling me how much she's looking forward to making a trip down to the Borromeo islands and maybe spending a morning at the market in Cannobio."

Sensing Max's embarrassment, Cai put his arm through Glain's and teased her: "You were reading the guide book all the way over on the flight... weren't you Mam?"

"Don't be so damn cheeky Cai," Glain said with a laugh in her voice. "I married your father but I was never your Mam. He's only eight years younger than me see, Max... I was married to a much older man."

"I'm sorry," Max said, laughing, "I'd just assumed that you were a couple." Cai sensed too that he was sorry for the way he'd flinched.

"Well, " Glain said, "we're on a 'singles' holiday... but it's so horrible to sit and eat on your own — or have to share a table with strangers who've never seen a fish knife in their lives. We decided to come away together, but to do our own thing and still have one another's company at meal times."

"I know exactly what you mean," Max confided. "This is my first holiday on my own... since the divorce."

"And are you planning to do all those touristy things then, Max... the islands and the Villa Taranto?" Cai quizzed, seeing a plan come together.

"Isn't that why people come to Lago Maggiore?" Max asked with a shrug.

"So maybe, when I go off hiking," Cai ventured, "you two might keep one another company?"

"And you could eat with us, Max," Glain said with an open

armed gesture that perhaps said more than she'd intended about her own wishful thinking. "We can be a ménage!"

"But are you sure I know how to use a fish knife?" Max quizzed, with a sparkle of mischief in his eyes.

When I first met Tudor he'd been on a fairly tough fitness regime for about a year. He was still big. When he took off his clothes you could see that he was still fat and that his skin was loose, even saggy, from where the five stones had been lost. He was older... quite a bit older really, but it didn't seem to matter. After we'd been together a couple of years he was down to thirteen stone and still working out. It was about that time that I became quite insecure for a while... once he'd got himself into such good shape and was looking like a film star. No fitness regime was going to sort out my face: no amount of kisses would make it better and we couldn't afford cosmetic surgery.

"It's quite a sight, don't you think?" Max volunteered as the boat turned towards the shore. "The people who recommended I come here said that the ferry was the best way to approach Cannero for the first time."

"It's beautiful... and that must be the Villa Cannero," Glain said, pointing at the yellow and white palace to the right of the jetty, its balconies heavy with pink geraniums, its lawned terraces stepped down to the water's edge.

"I think I'm going to be pleased that we paid for a balcony and a lake view," Cai said, remembering the argument he'd had with Glain over all the supplements; the single room surcharge alone was outrageous.

It took a long time for me to understand that Tudor loved me... perhaps because I don't know, even to this day, if I loved him. He said — once, when he was pissed off with me because I kept doubting him — that the chip on my shoulder was more repellent than the scar on my face... but that the chip, at least, was something I could work on.

After the last of the grand villas, high above the village, the cobbled track ended abruptly. Rough steps, hewn into the rock, led to a steep path that quickly yielded panoramas of the lake, which shimmered in the morning heat, taking Cai's breath away. The gradient soon exhausted his awe at the views and his startled amazement at the zucchini-fat lime-green lizards that skited into the undergrowth from sun-soaked slabs of granite. Stopping now and then for long draughts of rosemary-scented air, he watched butterflies — some a silky black, many more common yellows, and the rare few with blood red wing tips. He was amazed too by the hydrangeas — banks and banks purple, indigo and pink, like surreal cotton wool clouds that had fallen from the sky and come to rest on the mountainside.

After a three-hour climb, Cai ate bread and cheese, and drank some rough local wine, at an *osteria* in Cheglio. The youth that seemed to be in charge had a square face, although there were no hard corners. A light beard softened the lines of his jaw and waves of sun-streaked hair crested onto the wide strand of his forehead. When he smiled his cheeks puffed and his eyes danced: a lapis gem in the lobe of his right ear drew attention away from their gaze. His smile revealed beautiful teeth between lips that were fleshy. Cai watched him pout as he supped beer from a bottle. Then, distracted by another customer, the smile faded and the youth's face became too mean. Two or three times during the afternoon, as Cai climbed down the mountain, he thought about the smiling face.

One morning, after his shower, Tudor placed my fingers to the right and just below his left nipple. His muscles were hard anyway, after all the workouts, and I couldn't feel the lump he said he'd found.

Over dinner that evening, Max got carried away describing the palace gardens on Isola Bella and Glain sat and watched him, all dewy-eyed. When they carried their coffees out onto the terrace, Cai remained at the table, aware of the stiffness in his calves and thighs after the daylong hike. Stretching his legs gently, he watched Marco, the waiter who'd served them, and tried not to think about his aching muscles. Marco had that slight stoop of so many tall men; an apology for having his head stuck above the crowd or just a habit developed from too many bumps against beams and door lintels? His skin was dark against the whiteness of his shirt. Perhaps there were sculptured curves concealed within the crisp cotton — muscles toned at a gym or worked out in the early morning along the lengths of a pool — but he looked too lean for his own good. His hair was slicked and spiky, as seemed to be the season's fashion, and blacker than shoe polish. When he lifted his head he always wore a smile that evoked a sense of well-being… and doubtless elicited generous tips. Cai sensed the rousing in his body. It surprised and shocked him: such feelings had been quiet for so long. And he remembered how the memory of the youth who'd served him bread and cheese had come back to him. Lingering over his *espresso*, he wrestled with the sense that he was betraying Tudor… and held on to the vain hope that Marco's cheerful eyes would hold him in a cruisy gaze.

After seeing two specialists, there was an operation to remove his breast, some of the lymph nodes under his arm and part of the chest wall muscles. He never showed me the scar… never let me draw my fingers gently over it, or run my tongue along its length. He never let me kiss it better.

Straw-coloured curls, some darker and tighter — still wet from the shower — softened the angular lines of his youthful face. His pale lips, moist from the grapefruit juice, were pursed at the glass's rim, his thoughts momentarily distracted. Behind his hazel eyes, dreams were still being dreamed as everyone about him, except Cai, broke their fast with salami and cheese, strong black coffee and chocolate croissants. The sun broke from the clouds and drenched him in brightness. Perplexed by the surges in his body, Cai stared at the man: he looked like one of the angels in a painting Max had liked so much that he'd brought the Isola Bella brochure down to dinner the previous evening to show Cai what he'd missed. A little girl in a high chair, her face blotched with Nutella, began to cry. The curly haired man lifted her onto his lap, muttered something in what Cai thought might be Dutch and kissed her cheek with those moist lips. It was a kiss Cai longed to taste. Glain, too distracted by her infatuation with Max, failed to sense Cai's reawakening.

Then there were long months of chemotherapy... with puking, hair loss and despair. Some of the outer circle, in whom we'd chosen not to confide, assumed it was AIDS related. It was funny how their assumption sat so easily with Tudor and me. Men didn't get breast cancer.

From Laveno, Cai planned to take the open bucket cable lift to Sasso Fermo and hike for a few hours on the ridge, seven hundred metres above the lake. Next to him in the queue for the early morning ferry stood a man about his own age. Cai noticed his sunken cheeks, weighed down by slate-grey bags beneath eyes of smudged brown... and the bluish, keloid scar that cut across his chin for more than an inch. The man said something in Italian to the middle-aged woman in the ticket booth that must have been funny because she laughed loudly. A group of impatient students, English Tory-types, pushed into the queue besides Cai, distracting him and drawing the opprobrium of the middle-aged Germans further back on the line. The man with the bluish scar moved down the long jetty and was lost in the crowd.

Cai saw him again, standing at the rail of the boat looking back at Cannero; he swept back the strands of hair that had blown across his face with nervous flicks of his fingers. Now he looked less sombre, the suggestion of a smile on his face. Cai watched him with no conscious motive. After some time the man turned towards Cai, and as if he'd sensed Cai's interest, he nodded, said

"Ciao," and headed for the door that led into the bar.

About a year after we thought that everything was okay, the back pain started and the doctor said that perhaps he should have a scan.

He was standing with his elbow on the high counter, cigarette in hand, drinking an *espresso*. When he wasn't drinking, he rubbed the fibrous blotch on his chin with the thumb of the hand that held his cigarette, the smoke swirling about his face. Cai asked the girl, who looked too young to be a regular employee and was perhaps still at school and doing a summer job, for a bottle of mineral water.

"So, you're English," the man said to Cai, surprising him. "Do you want one?"

Cai looked at the open packet of Camels that was thrust towards him and wished that he smoked so that he'd have a reason to linger.

"I don't… but thanks," he said, sounding apologetic.

"I studied in Newcastle for a year; do you know it?"

"No, not well. I'm from north Wales… other side of the country."

"Ah… I climbed a mountain in Wales once, but I don't remember its name… too many consonants."

"Welsh is like that," Cai quipped with a smile.

"My name is Danilo Magistrini… my friends call me Dani."

And the scan showed a tumour on the spine, which the surgeon said was inoperable. Of course, none of them would say how long he'd got.

Caught in Cai's gaze, Dani finished his coffee and said, "Mine is from an accident when I was fourteen." A curl of smoke rose as he stroked the scar again. "I came off my brother's motorbike."

Cai didn't know what to say and in the moments of his hesitation he considered the palpable strangeness of the intimacy into which their scars had seduced them.

"I guess you haven't made friends with yours yet, then," Dani ventured.

Cai wanted to say, "Well, fuck you Dani Magistrini," but he remained silent and wondered what sort of friend got you noticed in such a way that you were scorned.

"I'm sorry, I didn't mean to offend you," Dani said, seeing something in Cai's face that Cai hadn't intended to give away.

"It's not offence I'm feeling," Cai said, and searched for words... but found none.

The two men looked at each other long enough for discomfort. In the moment before he turned to leave the bar, Cai wanted Dani to hold him.

Tudor didn't want to add months to life; he just wanted quality for the life that he had left. He wasn't religious, but he had this notion that all the advances of medicine had a lot to answer for: he wasn't going to allow his life, his spirit, to be held hostage in a rotting body that was past its use-by date. He thought that was a kind of idolatry. But he took all the pain relief they could offer him.

For a while, before climbing the steps that led to the ridge path, Cai watched the paragliders jump from Sasso Fermo's sheer cliff edge, into the void where the currents carried them out over the valley. The view across the lake aroused him... or perhaps it was Dani's kiss... and he felt more alive than he had in months.

At bedtime on the night that Tudor died, he kissed my scarred face to 'make it better' one last time.

High up on the ridge, Cai paused to catch his breath, drink some water and marvel at the view.

Glossary of Welsh terms that appear in these stories:

Just Beyond the Buddleia Bush
Cwningar – The Warren (literally rabbit warren)
pidyn - penis

A Particular Passion
Pobol y Cwm – A Welsh language soap opera
Cefn Gwlad – rural backwaters

Between the Devil and the Virgin
Nain – Grandmother
Craig y Forwyn – the virgin's rock
Craig y Cythraul – the devil's rock

Mischief and Deep Secrets
Capal Wesla – Wesleyan Chapel
Parchedig – Reverend

Gifts
Dewi-post – Dewi-the-postman

REVIEWS OF WELSH BOYS TOO:

"An interracial gay couple baby-sits the two young children of a friend for a weekend; a high school boy grapples with his emergent sexuality while looking for support from the conservative adults in his life; and a mentally disturbed woman seeks vengeance against the brother who slept with her husband, in John Sam Jones's **Welsh Boys Too**. These intriguing short stories look at homosexuality through the lens of Welsh culture, subtly linking homophobia to other kinds of discrimination – racism, religious intolerance – with objectivity and sensitivity."
Publisher's Weekly, March 12, 2001

"**Welsh Rarebit** - John Sam Jones's charming, thoughtful collection of Welsh stories, **Welsh Boys Too**, is a joy to read. Contemporary, yet timeless, these tales of young men living in rural Wales have a pathos and dignity to them that sustains this slim, but vibrant collection. Rustic homophobia tends to be insidious rather than blatant, and Jones's subtlety of language and style highlight this, as does the wild, unsophisticated backdrop of the slopes of Cader Idris, or the seagulls circling the cliffs of the barely inhabited island of Enlli. Unsophisticated these men may be, unscathed they are not – but they are survivors, and their stories are as uplifting as they are sad. Treat yourselves".
Sebastian Beaumont in *Gay Times*, London, March 2001

"**Welsh Boys Too** is a bold and adventurous collection of stories inspired by the lives of gay men in Wales. Funny, poignant and ultimately revealing, it introduces John Sam Jones as a new voice in the world of Welsh fiction. After spending years away from home, studying in California and as a chaplain in Liverpool, Jones returned to North Wales to be saddened by the prevailing homophobia within society and began, through writing, to explore the lives of the gay men who lived there. In a sequence of short, pointed stories, seen through the eyes of eight men, he discloses, in an often humorous manner, how they try to live their lives in a society where rejection is second nature."

The Western Mail, Cardiff, Saturday 9 December 2000

"...John Sam Jones has balanced this short anthology well; each story earns its space and does not take away from any of the other works presented. An example of this balance is the collection's ability not to shy away from sex whilst not sensationalising it either."

Adam Lewis in *Gair Rhydd*, Cardiff, November 2000

"Cymreictod ynddo'i hun yw un o'r Pethau sy'n ein gwneud ni'n fwy cul... ac mae'r iaith Gymraeg yn arf yn erbyn pobl hoyw. Dyna un rheswm pam fod Cymro Cymraeg wedi penderfynu cyhoeddi ei straeon byrion Cymreig eu naws yn uniaith Saesneg... Mae **Welsh Boys Too** gan John Sam Jones yn gasgliad o wyth stori fer sy'n trafod gwahanol agweddau o fywydau dynion hoyw yng Nghymru."

Cerys Bowen yn *Golwg*, Tachwedd 2000

The eight quite short stories in this thin yet evocative first-ever collection of queer fiction from Wales open the door, with fluid charm, on yet another culture's take on coming out, AIDS, homophobia and domestic togetherness. Though undeniably contemporary there is at the same time an other-worldliness to the author's world; the familiar is filtered through the gaze of a culture which is as distinct from that of America, or even England, as, for example, Italy's might be, or that of Greece. Makes for fiction that's both absorbing and entertainingly anthropological.

Richard Labonte
http://users.lanminds.com/qink/labonte/reviews.htm

From Booklist

Packing eight stories into a slim paperback, Jones is a paragon of economy. In the five-page "But Names Will Never Hurt Me," he gives us everything necessary to understand why the 17-year-old protagonist, who has already made his affectional choices, decides that "Rent boy . . . didn't sound so bad." In nine unhurried pages, "The Magenta Silk Thread" reveals exactly why a 77-year-old war widow is attending her best friend's son's wedding and taking the train rather than getting a lift to it. Altogether, these stories present a cross-section of a new embattled minority within an old one—Welsh gay men. Jones' examples embrace both terms of their identity. Several proudly speak Welsh, and all must come to terms with dour Welsh Calvinism as they do the public dance of appearances that being gay often requires. Jones makes them all vivid and sympathetic, not least by changing narrative perspective from story to story, from first-person subjective to third-person omniscient and even to second-person imperative. *Ray Olson*

£4.99   ISBN 1-902638-11-5   www.parthianbooks.co.uk

Marc Rees is one of Wales's leading exponents of contemporary dance. His innovative performances are known for flamboyant and humorous interpretations of history, culture and personal experience. In addition to working with some of the foremost physical theatre companies, his solo work includes *Iddo Ef*, *Caligula Disco*, *A Very Gladys Night* and *RevolUn*.

He has lived and worked in Holland and Germany and has been involved in international collaborations with artists, film-makers and choreographers across Europe and North America.

"Rees is part of a new generation of performers whose work is informed by an acute awareness of queerness as performance, of the way in which we act out, shape and re-shape our identities every day. Rees brings to this his own unique interest in how we are formed by the spaces in which we spend our lives. His work is driven by a desire to map out a new *milltir sgwâr* for himself in performance, a 'queer space' in which to live and work."

Heike Roms, *New Welsh Review*

For further information on the work of Marc Rees
www.r-i-p-e.co.uk